ROSE'S GIFT

RAIN TRUEAX

Rose's Gift

Arizona Historical Book 4
is an original work of Rain Trueax.
All rights reserved.

Echoes From The Past sample included

Prepared and presented by:
Seven Oaks
Monmouth, Or.

INTRODUCTION

Some say life is a cycle, but it's really a spiral. Seasons come and go, but when they return, it's to a new place.

A sixty year old widow, Rose has her life set out in a comfortable way-- bridge, tea with friends, family dropping by, and a nice little home. She went through a depression when she lost her husband four years earlier but has come to terms with life as it must be—or so she thought, until a man comes along to challenge her assumptions.

Ollie, nearly sixty, has been cowboy, rustler, and ranch foreman. When he saw something he wanted, he has come to Tucson to claim it. Knowing more about cattle and horses than women, he set out to woo Rose by showing her the kind of man he is.

Except, is it too late? Can she give up her comforts? This man won't be satisfied with living in the city as she has. She will have to change more than adding a man to her bed... He has made it clear what kind of marriage he intends it to be. Is she up to that? Accepting his proposal could upset his friends and hers. A new life? A new home? A wedding? A happily ever after? Or is it all too late?

From the first three Arizona historicals, the novella, *Rose's Gift* brings together characters for a birth, a death, and a wedding-- all in the holiday season. Change is on its way. None of them are ready for it, but ready or not, here it comes.

CHAPTER 1

It was the year of our Lord, 1900, a year that Rose had begun without any feeling it would be different than the years before it, all the years since her husband had died in 1896. An old woman, Rose had thought she would end her life sooner than she had. What was with that? Can't a body even die when it's the right time? At sixty, she was feeling far less old than she'd been expecting. She shook her head. Silly old woman.

She walked to the door and stepped onto her porch, shaking out the dust mop. She missed Holly. The girl was so full of life, had added so much zest to her days. She understood though that when her father died, Holly had to return to Chicago to help her sister take care of the estate—it was apparently complicated and sizable one.

Knowing Grace, who was like a granddaughter to her, was expecting her baby in November could accounted for her feeling of youthfulness-- except it didn't. She looked across the yard and saw the reason her heart was beating faster.

He leaned on a shovel and smiled at her. He had thrown his shirt over the nearby fence. His skin was slick with sweat. He was a tall man, looked to be skinny but without his shirt, she saw he was all ropy muscle-- lean and strong for a man who had to be in his late fifties. He took off his hat, showing the balding head, which he wiped with the handkerchief he'd pulled from his back pocket.

"You need somethin' Mz. Redman?" he asked with that faint smile and those keen blue eyes that had her barely resisting a sigh.

"No, just. Would you like some lemonade, Mr. Oliver? Looks to me like you have the garden pretty well dug up."

"Just a little more. I was thinkin' though that I oughta take out that old cottonwood. I know you like it but look at its leaves this year, see the rot in its trunk. It's gonna fall over in a wind one of these days. Could land in your parlor."

"But Mr. Oliver, how could you take it out safely? The very danger you expressed is my concern about having anyone cut it down."

"Just gotta know the right way, ma'am. I can do it if you want."

She considered that. She didn't doubt he had the strength with those muscles. What if it split or fell on him.

"Please come in for some lemonade, and we can... talk about it. I made some sugar cookies."

"I'm too dirty and sweaty for that, ma'am. Maybe bring them outside on the porch?"

She shook her head. "That's silly. It's much cooler in the house. It's not as though a little dirt or sweat will hurt

2

my home." She turned and walked in, unsure if he would follow. She knew one thing though. She wanted him to follow. She wanted to see him sitting at her table. She wanted them to talk about something, about anything. She didn't remember the last time she had felt this way about a man, about wanting a man sitting at her table. Of course, there had been that feeling with James, but it had been so many years ago, that it wasn't a thought or feeling anymore. It just was a distant memory.

A moment later, he opened the door. His shirt was on and buttoned but not tucked in. "You can wash up at the sink," she said. He went to it and rolled up his sleeves before washing his hands and forearms. She tried to look away from those long-fingered hands as he rubbed the soap over them and then over his forearms before rinsing with fresh water. As he dried his skin, she saw the muscles working under its surface. She asked herself again—what is this? Whatever it was, she was way too old for it.

He'd been a guest in her home many times. First, he had come with the family for which he worked, friends of hers who lived in the San Rafael Valley miles to the south of Tucson. He had been sick and only reluctantly agreed to medical help. When he was stronger, she had thought she'd not see him again-- ranch hands didn't get to town often. It surprised her when her friend Connie told her that he had returned and was now living in Tucson. Not long after, he began coming around with an offer to do chores.

She shook her head in an attempt to clear it. She was being idiotic. She poured him cold lemonade from her icebox. It and the house had been a gift from Cilla.

Rose regretted her inability to have children with James, but Cilla had been so much like a daughter and later Grace like a granddaughter that it taken away the sting. A woman could be a mother by ways other than natural birth. Soon she'd be helping Grace become one. Maybe even someday Holly would return and have babies. Rose could be a grandmother or even great grandmother-- if not of blood, of the heart. She smiled.

"What are you thinking about, gal?" Ollie asked staring at her over the rim of his glass. He had yet to take one of the cookies.

"My girls. I've been a fortunate woman."

"Reckon it's been the same for me," he said as he sipped the lemonade. "Sam's my kin as much as if it was by blood."

"He calls you his mother."

"Don't mind. Sure, I look after him... or did."

"I was surprised when you left the ranch. I know how much you love him."

"I had my reasons." He leaned back in the chair, tilting the legs a little, as men were wont to do.

"I appreciate all you have done for me here."

He set the chair firmly on its feet. His gaze met hers without wavering. "You know why, I reckon."

She ran her tongue over her lips. My god what was this about? She was tempted to look away, but she could not. She was too old for this. She was...

"It was you, Rose. I can call you Rose, can't I?"

She nodded. "Of course."

"They call me Ollie, but it ain't my name. Would you be wanting to call me by my given name?"

Her smile felt weak. "I would like that."

"It's Roman. Now don't you be telling anybody else that. Nothing wrong with it. I ain't wanted for anything under it. Just not much of a name for an ugly old coot like me."

"Ugly?"

"Like a big old vulture or maybe heron. Big nose, not much hair on top, just a skinny old man. I got no right to be thinking what I am, but guess I also ain't never been a man to walk away from something before I know I have to. I also know you fork a horse as soon as you get to him to make him know what you mean to do... not that I meant..." His smile was crooked. For the first time she knew he had a sense of humor and could laugh at himself.

"You're not ugly to me, Roman," she said. "I guess you have Italian in your family for that first name."

He shrugged. "Don't know much about my family. They never talked about the past, too busy trying to survive the present. Kansas... well, it was always a battle-field-- long as I knew it for anything. Everybody wanted a piece of it, and slavery was dividing the territory long afore it got to the whole nation. Ever hear of the Pottawatomie Massacre?"

"No. Oh, maybe I had. I was born in Missouri. It was divided over slavery also. What happened?" She wanted to ask how it had affected him, but maybe he wouldn't want to talk about that.

"They come at night. May 24th, 1856. John Brown, the murdering bastard, and a bunch of his abolitionists. They murdered five settlers that they thought or were told were pro-slavery. They used broadswords. Just massacred 'em as the ones they hit in the dark didn't have a chance to fight back. Our home was one of their targets. I wasn't home. I'd got a job working at the fort, wrangling horses."

"How old were you?"

"Fourteen. I wish I'd been home though. Should've been home."

"What could you have done?"

His smile was cold. "More than from where I was. They murdered my pa. He was not pro-slavery, not that anybody asked or cared. Brown just wanted to stir up war."

"Did the law then hang the killers?"

Ollie's smile turned cynical. "You have a lot of faith in the law, gal?"

"Of course."

This time he laughed. She was surprised to realize how much she liked his laugh even when it was sarcastic. "That time they got away. Brown though was a fanatic. He kept up his work of stirring up war. Harper's Ferry was his downfall and yeah, he got hung then but not for what he did in Kansas."

"It was a terrible time for families. And the rest of yours?"

"From then on my working wasn't a choice. I signed on with different outfits. Mama got the fever and died the winter of '58. Kansas was torn up then for the next ten years... more with the outlaw gangs."

"Did you fight in the war?"

"Sign up to kill innocent folks? Nah. I wasn't someone they could conscript either. Moved around too much."

"When did you meet Sam?"

"He was a kid and on his own. My God, he was a tough little nut but then if he hadn't been, with life like it'd been for him, he'd have not lived to grow up. He said he wanted to be my pard. I laughed but ya know what, he was and we been pards, him the boss and me the mom, wal until earlier this year."

"You love him like a son."

"I do. Like you love Cilla, but even a mama's got to let her son go someday." His smile was more real.

"And that's why you came to Tucson, to let Sam go?"

He rose then and walked around the table to take her hands and draw her to her feet. "You know that ain't so, don't you?"

She felt tears in her eyes. She did know it. It was terrible to feel this. It was so unfaithful to James.

"Your husband was a good man, Rose, but he's been dead now four years. If there's a reason this can't happen between us, it's not him. It's how you feel about me."

He was so direct. In that he was like James, but in so many other ways she knew he wasn't. He'd been an outlaw. He'd ridden with a gun, still carried one most of the time. He'd led a past that she couldn't even imagine. James had been a gentle man, strong, even tough when needed, but they were nothing alike. Still, James had liked Ollie... Roman. She looked up then and met his gaze.

"I don't ask you to give me an answer right now, Rose," he said using a tone she'd never heard from him before, "but I want you to know the way I am thinking. If there is no chance for me, I want you to be honest. I'll still be a friend to you." He dropped her hands but didn't move away.

"I do need to think. I hadn't expected." Maybe she

had, but it was more dream than expectation. Could this be real?

"I want you to know I have money. I ain't coming to you broke. I've worked all my life. Yeah, some of it bordered on dishonest, if you want to be hard-line on the cattle we brought back from Mexico to sell to ranchers, but I didn't break laws in this country. I have enough money to provide you a home, for us to live a good life."

"Well, I have this home for all my living days. Cilla bought it for me." What had she said? She was seriously considering the practical aspects of doing this.

"I am a man of the desert, of the land, gal. I need more space around me than this home of yours, nice as it is. Would you be willing to think about that too?"

She felt her mouth drop open. This was all so much to take in. She had her bridge friends. There was Connie to visit. "Where would you want to go?"

"Wal, when I got to Tucson, I bought a piece of land. It's out toward the Catalinas. Nice view of the valley from its ridge. Pretty piece of desert. Fair soil. I started building a home up there soon as I got here. I've hired a crew to work with me. Cordova helped me find good people."

"Rafe?"

"His father, Raul. I asked them both to keep it quiet. Because Maria is your friend, it wasn't possible for him to work on it without her knowing and maybe telling you. I wasn't ready for you to know. He did though find the materials, even helped me work out a plan for this climate and that piece of land. Nobody knows building like Cordova."

"I am shocked."

She saw he had to work for a smile. "I'll fence a

garden space and plant some fruit trees. Soon I'll have a water tank to catch the rain, store the overflow from the stream that comes out of the mountains most of the year. I will make it nice for you, Rose."

"You know it wouldn't be about the home," she said as she moved to the stove and tried to think what he was saying.

"I understand. You need to get to know me better, to feel good about this. I will give you time. Even court you proper if you want."

"You want..."

"I won't ask you now because I know it's too soon, but you need to know what I want. I want you to be my wife, Rose Redman."

She moved back to the table and sat down. Shock washed over her. It was all so much, so fast. "It's actually Rose Jarrod Redman." She smiled; even though she was still undecided if this made sense.

He grinned. "Roman Alexander Oliver."

"Goodness."

"A mouthful all right. Ollie is easier. You call me that... Wal, except in one instance."

She looked up as he moved to the door. "I didn't mean this to be a platonic marriage, Rose."

She gave him a look.

He smiled. "Ya know what I mean. I waited a long time for a woman like you. I want you to be sure that it's what you want too." With that he was gone.

Rose walked quickly down the street and entered Sicilla's store. Connie came from the back. "What's wrong," she asked, as she took Rose's arm and urged her into Del and her private quarters.

Rose shook her head and tried to think how to say what was on her heart. "Not wrong. Well, maybe it is wrong."

Connie nodded, took some tea leaves from a box before moving to the stove and pouring steaming water into the kettle. She looked back at Rose and then smiled. "My goodness, I can't believe it. You are in love. How did this happen?"

"I thought you didn't do readings without permission," Rose said with a note of what she knew was annoyance in her voice. Unfair or not, she didn't want Connie doing readings for her, to know things she didn't know herself.

Connie giggled. "Don't need to. You are flushed, acting nervous as a girl. I've never actually seen you look so young, my friend. You are in love. Who is it?"

"I'm not in love. I'm... in confusion."

"Talk to me then." She brought the teapot to the table and went back for two china cups.

Del came to the door. "Mary Richter is out there. You want me to take care of your side of the store?" He smiled. "Okay, I'll do that." He disappeared.

"Now, tell me," Connie said as she put a small plate of cookies on the table and sat down.

"It's foolishness is what it is."

"Tell me anyway."

"Ollie asked me to marry him."

Connie's mouth dropped open. "Mr. Oliver, the foreman for Sam Ryker's ranch?"

"Yes." She felt relieved that Connie had not been looking into her personal affairs. She wasn't sure how much power Connie really had, but she preferred they approach each other evenly... unless, of course, she asked for advice.

Connie was silent a moment. "And you said?"

"I was in shock. I said nothing."

"You have feelings for him?"

Rose managed a smile. "It seems unfair to James."

"In what way? He's dead. Do you think he'd want you to stay alone?"

'No, of course not, but... Well, we shared so much, and we wouldn't be sharing this."

Connie poured them each a cup of tea. "How do you know?"

"You think he knows?"

"The other side isn't so far as you think."

Rose took a sip of the tea. "Well... er uh... what does he think about it then?"

"You want me to ask?"

She considered that a moment before, with a little trepidation, she nodded. "Can you?"

"I can only try. It doesn't always work, you know."

Rose felt foolish, but she nodded again. "Try."

Connie reached out and took her hand before she lowered her head. There was such a long silence that Rose began to think it wouldn't work.

"I am asking James Redman to come and visit with us if he is of a mind to do so," Connie said as she squeezed Rose's hand.

It was a longer silence before Connie said, "Rose, do you know someone called Ruth?"

Rose felt a shock run through her. "That was my grandmother's name."

"She is the one who has come to me. She seems to be a bit of a wizard herself, Was she?"

Rose smiled. "Sometimes I thought so."

"Well, she is here. She said... Let me see if I got this right. Something more is coming and you and Roman Oliver will meet it together. It will be good if you love him. But she said... Be sure you do love him. You will need to love him if this is to work."

"I don't understand."

Connie shook her head. "She didn't say more." She looked up. "She smiled though. She looks rather like you but with red hair."

"Her hair was silver when I knew her, but... it had been red."

"I think she found it all amusing. It will be all right, Rose, if you care for him. Only you can decide that."

"James though didn't come?"

"They don't always. Sometimes they have already been reborn. Sometimes they are off somewhere or maybe not removed enough to want to come back. It's not a bad sign that he didn't come."

Rose sighed. "Then it's up to me."

"And what you feel for the man."

That was the issue.

CHAPTER 2

Rose chose a simple blue dress with a white collar, almost Puritan style. She knew why she was doing that. She was not a sexual woman anymore. Had she ever been?

Looking at herself in the mirror, she saw the gray that was working to take over her blonde hair. She sighed. How many times had she sighed since Ollie had blown her world apart? She could not count them.

If she had hoped Connie would find her an answer from James, she had been disappointed. It was up to her. Could she really love another man? She had met James when she was a girl, married him at seventeen. She had never thought of another man that way, as it had always been him. With the years, their relationship had changed into one more of friendship than passion. Not having children had colored their years, but then they had come to work for the Wesleys, and Priscilla had been the daughter they never had, her children their grandchildren. Was it a real life or only in fantasy? No, love made it real.

James was no longer able to be in her life. He had fought to live but finally died of a lingering illness that had drained both their energies before he finally had released his hold on this life.

The knock at the door stopped her ruminating. Was Ollie going to demand an answer she didn't yet have? She opened the door and managed a smile. He was wearing a shirt she had never seen and had a bouquet of flowers in his hand. She stepped aside to let him enter her parlor. When Grace had entertained her beaus there, she had never imagined she might do the same.

"I am sorry, Rose," he said as he handed her six red roses before he sat on the sofa. "I came on too sudden. I should've not pushed you like I did. I was acting like an unbroke colt."

She held onto the roses. It had been years since anyone had given her any. Had they ever? She dropped into a chair across from him. She should put the roses in water. She didn't want to release them. "I didn't feel you did that."

"I just... Wal, getting to my age, I don't see the years in front of me that I left behind. I was rushin' ya and I didn't mean to do that."

"Are you taking back your question?" she asked meeting his gaze levelly.

"Not at all. Just figured I should do some courtin', not expect ya to just know what ya want the way I did."

She knew suddenly. It was such a shock to realize how much she did know. She only had one question first.

"Do you like me?"

He gave a little laugh. "What's not to like? I like you a lot. You take care of those around you, offer loving touches to everybody, you cook real good, you think, and I like a woman who can think. Yes, I like you."

"All right... if you really do want me to marry you, the answer is yes."

He smiled then. It was at first a small smile but then a broader one. "You will be my wife?"

She nodded.

"Then, come sit here on the sofa with me, gal."

"Why?" But she knew.

"I told ya what I wanted. I want to give you a little taste of it."

She fought back tears as she rose and moved to sit on the sofa, not too close. "I might need time. It's been awhile." It had been forever.

He moved to sit closer to her. He took the roses from her hand and set them on the side table before he reached out and took her chin in his hand. His fingers had a roughness to them that of a working man with calluses. His touch was gentle. "Can I kiss you?" he asked.

"It would be all right." More than all right, as she felt her heart begin to race. Could this be happening to her?

He bent his head toward her and lightly brushed her lips with his. When she thought that would be all, he pushed his tongue against her lips and delved within her mouth. My God, what was that? James had never... She suddenly lost all track of what had been as she was lost in the sensation of his tongue brushing hers, the kiss deepening as he pulled her into his arms. Her body awoke to feelings she had never known.

When he released her, he moved back just enough to

meet her gaze with his own clear blue eyes. "I've wanted to do that since the first day I saw you," he whispered as he bent and brushed her cheek with his lips. "You were married then and I stopped myself from thinking that way. Then when I heard your husband died, I wanted to give you time. I didn't want to rush you. Anything worth having is worth waiting and working for. But was the kiss... was it too much?"

He was so sensitive. She hadn't expected that. She lifted her hand to his shoulders and felt the solid muscle moving under her fingers. She managed to shake her head. "I just... I don't know much about..." She didn't want to admit all she didn't know much about. It might make him think less of James or of her.

He smiled. "I don't either," he said. "Not of this kind of feeling. We can learn together."

Tears ran down her cheeks.

"My God," he said as he brushed one away. "Is this making you unhappy?"

"No, it's... I can't explain it. Just it's too much."

"I can come back another day."

"No." She put her arms around him, holding him now as tightly as he had held her. "Don't go away. It's too much in a good way."

"How soon will you be my wife?" he asked.

"I can't do it before Grace has her baby. After her miscarriage, well even though this pregnancy has gone well, she needs me."

"And I want the house ready for you."

"Will you let me see it?" she asked running her finger lightly down his cheek, liking the roughness of his beard.

"Of course, and you can tell me what you want."

"The baby is due in November. Then comes Christmas. I think the whole family will be here for that."

She felt his smile against her cheek as he bent again to kiss her lightly. "I want you to be sure, not be hurried about this. How about Valentine's Day?"

She laughed and moved back. "That's a kind of sentimental day for a cowpoke, isn't it?"

"We can be sentimental too. This though is also practical. I will never forget the anniversary that way." His smile made her smile. This time his kiss claimed her lips, and the feelings it aroused went all through her body. Three months. That would be a long time to wait for...

"I better go," he said as he arose and pulled her to her feet. "If I don't, I might not be willing to."

She knew then as surely as she had known anything in her entire life. "We are not children, Roman." It was the first time she had used his name. She saw by his smile that he liked it.

"No, we are a long way from children, which is why I should go."

"I mean... Well, we don't really have to wait for a wedding to... Well, you know." She could hardly believe she had said that. He would think she was a loose woman. Heavens, she was a loose woman.

"You saying what I think?" he asked his gaze steady on her.

"You are probably renting a hotel room. That is costly. I mean, you could stay here."

He laughed then. "No, I am not staying in a hotel."

"With a friend?" She felt confused.

"I sleep where I am building the house for us. The home I hoped would be for us."

"In a tent?"

"Don't need a tent."

She could hardly believe it. Sleeping out in the open. And it had rained earlier in the week. "Well that settles it." She looked down, seeing only the buttons on his shirt.

"You want me to stay here in a guest room?" he asked. He reached out and tipped up her chin to meet his gaze. She had never realized how blue his eyes were, how intense his gaze. Those eyes pulled her right into him.

"I wasn't thinking that would be necessary." She knew she was blushing as she saw he was smiling. He wrapped his arms around her. Those arms were strong, wiry; his body seemed all muscle. What kind of man was this?

"You don't care what people might think?" he asked. "What about your friends?"

"It is our business, not theirs. Besides most of them will be jealous."

"I'd marry you tomorrow with the judge if you were willing."

"I would like to have it be a party, a celebration. I like the idea of Valentine's Day. I am... Well, I know what I want now. And there is no reason for you to stay out on the desert at night."

"Rose, I am a man who's been without a woman for a long time. If I stay here, you know what it will mean?" He held her back from him so that he could look at her face.

She was the one to smile at his stern expression. "I think I do. Do you want to go out and get your things? Dinner will be ready at seven."

He smiled then. "I'll be back." In moments, he was out the door. She could almost imagine nothing had happened... except it had. Her whole world had changed.

It had been a long time since she had made love. She and James had fallen into a comfortable routine that didn't leave much room for deviation. Then he was ill, and they stopped sharing a bed. it had been almost five years and even longer since she had made love to a man. Or rather had sex. She wasn't sure that what she and James did qualified as making love.

She wondered how it would be with Ollie. Then she felt herself flush again as she imagined possibilities. She wasn't ignorant about sex, just mostly inexperienced. The one thing she knew for sure was, impulsive or not, she did not want to until Valentine's Day to find out what it would be like. Maybe it would be a disappointment, but she needed to know. She hoped he'd not be too tired when he returned. With that, she hurried into the kitchen to get dinner started.

Lying in bed, wrapped in Ollie's arms, Rose heard the chimes of the grandfather clock-- four. She could hardly believe the night they had had. How many times had they made love? She smiled against his bare chest. Three times. She'd never made love three times and climaxed each of them. He was a talented lover, surprising her with his sexual appetite and readiness to do what would please her as well as him.

"You are thinking," he whispered against her hair.

"And you are awake."

"Generally get up early... though not always after such a hard night." He chuckled.

"Maybe you should stay in bed today," she said before

she thought what that might mean and felt herself blushing.

"Not sure I'd get more rest that way." He brushed her hair back from her forehead and kissed it lightly. "Might be a good way to die though."

"Don't you dare say that," she protested.

"Heard a man can die that way. Be a good way for a man."

"Not for the woman."

She liked his laugh. "Then I won't do it. Got a good heart. Doc said so last time I saw him."

"You didn't used to like doctors."

"Still don't... except that one. He's all right."

She ran her fingers over his chest. The muscles felt good as they moved a little. He was only lightly haired in the center of his torso. She liked that too. A hairy man wasn't appealing to her.

"Still thinking too much."

"Well I did wonder about something."

"Okay."

"You said you have never been married."

"And that is true."

"Well, you are very good at... pleasing a woman."

She could feel his smile against her cheek. "And you wonder how I'd know that if I wasn't with a woman. Wal, not being married don't mean I been a monk."

"I can tell that... well I guess I can tell that." She felt embarrassed again.

"Not a lot of women though, Rose. And none for a lot of years. I had a good teacher though... long time back. She was a married woman, older'n me. First I thought she just wanted chores done, but then there was somethin' more. It was her taught me about lovemaking, how it should be for a woman."

"She was married... That's... adultery."

He lay back on the pillow and propped his hands under his head. "Yep. I was sixteen when it started. I wasn't thinkin' much about what it was back then. Her husband was older, wasn't around much. I guess you could say she seduced me past thinkin' about what it meant. Leastwise for awhile."

"Then you ended it?"

He made a thoughtful sound with his lips. "Nope. Young buck like I was, I wanted her. She ended it. Got me fired off the place. Taught me some about women right there."

"Not to be trusted?"

He nodded. "Not to care too much about any of 'em. I went from job to job for awhile, hooked up with Sam. Kansas was bein' torn up between the War and Jayhawkers."

"How old was he?"

"Almost eleven was what we figured. You know about Sam's ma being a whore. At least that's what he figured she was until later when he met Cord and learned otherwise about them having the same pa and... Life sometimes is pretty ugly."

"It can be." She had led a sheltered life in about every way that counted, but she knew how it was for others.

"Anyway, I was older. Still young to take on being a mama, but he needed somebody. Sam grew up faster than most and was a hellion even then."

"And you got into rustling later."

"Lots later. To begin it was riding for one brand or

another. But when you're young and randy, good with a gun, it's easy to slip from one thing to another. Never did nothin' in the States though, leastwise that we could get arrested for."

She smiled at that. "Other than bringing up stolen cattle."

"Other than." He pulled her back into his arms. She felt his smile against her temple. She liked how his mustache brushed her skin right before his lips. James had been a clean-shaven man. She discovered she liked facial hair. She remembered then how many ways she liked it and felt herself reddening again.

"Was..." He stopped. "Was I pushing you too much last night? You know what I mean? Didn't mean to hurt you if..."

"So it's your turn to think now," she teased.

"I lost my head, should've gone slower."

She laughed. "Roman, last night was wonderful for me. Like a dream I never knew I had. Don't you dare apologize for one moment of it."

She felt his smile again. "It was even more than that for me." He sucked in a breath. "I never made love before with a woman I loved. I never even knew how different that would be until last night."

She liked that. "How old are you?" She knew she was probably older but wondered how much—not that it was going to change anything now. She was as committed to him as if they had had the words already said over them.

"Born in '42. I'll be 59 by the time we get married."

"I was born in '40. I'll still be 60 but not by much. I was born in May."

"Me the middle of January."

"I am glad you are not a lot younger than me."

"Wouldn't matter. I started out with an older woman, reckon I like the idea of finishing with one... the right one this time." He raised himself over her. "And if last night wasn't too much for the right one... what do you think of sex before breakfast?"

"I think I should find out." She met his kiss now with her own tongue ready to play. She had a lot to learn and was eager to do it.

For Rose, the next weeks flew by with Grace's baby, Donovan, coming right on schedule. Grace, with the loving support of her husband, Rafe, proved to be a natural mother. Although Ollie now lived with Rose, she had not told the family. She was unsure how they would take the news.

She made many trips up to the site of what would be their new home. Raul was there twice and smiled when they both came, making his excuses, to leave them to look around together.

She loved the adobe, the view of mountains and desert. He had planned it with sheltering verandas that allowed for more windows, which almost made the desert seem part of the home. Behind the house, he fenced off a garden space and hired one of Raul's friends to bring up topsoil from the river bottom to make it even better for growing. There seemed to be nothing he would not do to make her life into all she could want.

Although there were no homes close to theirs, it wasn't much of a walk down the trail to a few others. She liked knowing that for the first time she would be mistress of her own home as the small house in Tucson always felt like it was Priscilla's.

She and Ollie were comfortable with each other, and the passion was sizzling, surprising her that a woman of sixty could feel such things. It was however, a delightful surprise. Whenever she heard his boots on the porch, her heart would beat faster, just like a girl's. She had seen others with that look on their faces, and she knew now it was on hers. All she had to do was get to Christmas when she would tell her family the news.

"And will you tell Sam when they are up for Christmas?" she asked Ollie as she was picking up the dishes from dinner.

"I guess I will." He gave a little laugh as he went to the sideboard and poured them each a brandy. "Not that he's got a say in this."

"Won't you want him to stand up with you when we are married?" She sat back at the table and sipped the brandy, a pleasant habit they had made their own each night.

"I'll ask him, o' course."

"I want it to be Priscilla for me... if she's willing."

"You worried about that? Damn, Rose. I don't want to do anything that's going to cause you trouble."

"Isn't it too late for that?" She smiled tentatively. Was he having second thoughts?

"I ain't going nowhere if that's what you're askin'. Just I don't want to make you unhappy."

"You won't. You haven't. I love you, Mr. Oliver and no

matter what the family thinks, our family by choice, not by blood, I want to be Mrs. Oliver."

He bent forward and kissed her. "Good. We'll work it out with them all. Sam should be glad about it. He's sure crazy enough about being married to Abby. He should understand me wanting some of the same thing. Minus the children, of course."

"It would have been nice to have had children though, wouldn't it? Just one of those things I missed."

"With the life I have led, it wasn't possible. Then Sam and Abby had Davy and Alice, which was good. I got some of what it felt like."

"Did they make you nervous, the babies that is?"

"Nah, I like the little ones. Just there was something somewhere else I wanted more." His sensual smile took her breath away. He did know how to say the words-- especially for a cowboy. Of course, she hadn't known many of them; so maybe he wasn't that unusual. She realized how she had come totally to think of him as Roman and would have to watch how she referred to him when she told her girls what was coming. He might not mind her calling him Roman, but he didn't appear as open to hearing it from others.

"Shall we tell them before Christmas or after?" she asked as her mind went back to the original worry.

"Unless we don't both go to Grace's for dinner, how would we put it off?" he asked with another of those grins that turned her into jelly.

"The girls were coming here for lunch as soon as Abby got into town. I can tell them then when they are together."

"Sam and Cord were going to help Rafe with branding; so guess it's as good a time as any for me to tell them while together. Likely they'll laugh."

"You think so?"

"I would've... a year ago." He reached for her and pulled her onto his lap. "Not laughing now though."

CHAPTER 3

R ose stared at the image in the mirror as she tried to steady her nerves. When had those lines appeared around her eyes? The silver in her hair had grown until it was all she saw as she pulled the lengths of hair up into a tight bun, securing it with pins.

"How can I possibly be thinking..." But she was. She was as giddy as a girl and now just as nervous. How had he come to her and changed everything in a heartbeat? Ollie. Oh my god, just saying his name had her feeling heat in parts of her body that she thought had gone dead. Dormant. She had been dormant, never expecting to come back alive.

When he had kissed her goodbye before he rode out to the ranch to do his own revealing, she knew how very alive she was to life, to her own body. How would she explain that to someone else? She had avoided telling her friends in town because it wasn't their business. It was the business of the three women, who would soon be sitting around her table as they had so many times. She needed to find the right words. It would likely be a shock.

Rose thought back to how she had felt her own life disappearing after James died. She had so little she had cared about or thought mattered. There had been nothing to want. She had been lost in a kind of fog where nothing mattered. She had begun to wake when Grace had stayed with her for a few weeks and then had come Holly—also giving new life, maybe making her ready for what was coming. He hadn't been much like a hero on a white horse, though he forked a horse just fine. She smiled as she remembered how forking a horse had been another expression he had taught her.

She took a deep breath and ran her hands down her hips, smoothing the fabric of her skirt. This was right. She knew it was. With renewed determination, she went into the kitchen and began preparing lunch as she waited for their arrival.

An hour later, the four of them were in her kitchen, Grace having opened her bodice and put her son to her breast. "All right, Aunt Rose, I know something is up. What is it?"

Rose managed a nervous smile. One thing she could count on with Grace is that she would confront whatever was in her way. Grace's determination helped her steady her nerves. She walked to the stove and took the tea kettle to pour water into the china pot where she had already placed Connie's special blend of tea.

She turned then-- no use in putting this off. She had practiced what she hoped were the right words—except were there any? Might as well bite the bullet, as her lover would say. She turned to face them with the pot in her hands. "I am getting married."

There was a moment of stunned silence.

"How could that be?" Cilla asked but managed a smile. "Not that I disapprove or anything but... who?"

"No reason you should not," Abby said rising to take the cups from the sideboard. "James has been dead a number of years. You should not be alone forever if you have found someone you can love now."

"I am glad you feel that way," Rose said as she brought the pot to the table and sat.

"When are you doing this and more importantly, who is it?" Cilla asked still staring at her with uncertainty in those big blue eyes.

"He's a good man, stable, wise, and younger than me by a few years," she said as she poured their tea.

"Why aren't you telling us his name?" Grace asked as she laid her son into the small crib in the corner of the kitchen.

"I will. Just I was... well, I was thinking it will be a bit of a shock."

Abby laughed. "Oh come on, Rose. Not that much of one. Who is it? Doc Hadley?"

Rose laughed with her. "No, it's not George... It's Roman Oliver."

"Who?" Abigail asked with an expression on her face that clearly bespoke shock.

"Ollie."

"Roman's his first name?" Abby whitened.

She nodded. "He is not comfortable with it." He said he never had been until he heard her whispering it after he kissed her. She flushed remembering those kisses.

"I am having a hard time grasping this," Abby said taking a gulp of tea.

"You are in love?" Cilla asked with an equal expression of shock.

"Surprisingly so, very much."

"And getting married," Abby repeated, shaking her head.

"Our plan is for Valentine's Day. We would like you all to be there. I know it's not easy to get up here to Tucson at that time of the year—ranch work and all; so will understand if it's not possible."

"It's not so much that," Abby said with a deep sigh as she stared into her tea.

"And this is why you asked us here today," Grace said. "I am thinking, even though it's early in the day, a little brandy might be in order. Of course, not for me. I don't want Donovan with a hangover." She grinned.

The long-time friends sipped their tea in a poignant silence before Abby sighed. "I am having a hard time grasping this."

"I understand."

"Ollie just seems... well seemed, too set in his ways."

Cilla laughed then. "It would appear not. I admit I am also surprised, but this is just another joining of our families. Like when we found out my Cord and your Sam were half brothers."

"This is a little different." Abby sipped her tea again before she pushed a recalcitrant strand of hair into a bun that looked ready to fall apart.

"Not all that much. I mean it surprises me too, but now that I think about it, it makes sense."

"When Ollie said he was going to live in Tucson, Sam and I thought it was his teeth or health or..."

"And instead, he was in courting mode." Cilla rose and moved to the sideboard where Rose had some pottery with interesting red and black designs. Cilla ran her fingers over the edge. "Did Holly give you these?" she asked before she reached into the cupboard for the brandy and three glasses.

"They had been in one of the ruins. I have no idea which one."

"Did she know about you and Ollie?"

"He hadn't asked me before she left to help take care of her father's affairs. I wrote two weeks ago to see if she could return for the wedding. I got her letter this morning. She said she wasn't surprised one bit. She hadn't said anything to me because she felt it would all be clear soon enough... I guess you all feel I am too old for a romance and new husband."

Grace laughed. "Don't include me in the too old business or even age difference. Rafe is older than me, but age is just a number."

"That is what he... Ollie says," Rose agreed with a smile.

"Well, you're not that much older," Abigail said as she obviously worked to get her head around this whole idea. Her eyes were troubled. "It's not that. I am being selfish. I don't want to lose Ollie."

"You aren't losing him. You are gaining her," Cilla argued. "It ties our families even closer together."

"Except, we always thought he would. That is, this means he won't come back to the ranch," Abby lamented.

"No, he probably won't," Cilla said with another

smile, "but you come here often these days—now especially that Grace and Rafe have a baby. If David wants to go away to school, that will also change things."

"I don't like change," Abigail said with a grimace.

"You are getting old, my friend."

She shook her head but managed a laugh. "We both are."

"Agreed."

"All right." She looked at Rose. "So who tells Sam?"

"Roman probably is doing that right now."

"Are we supposed to call him Roman now?" She forced a smile.

"Only if you want to get punched," Rose said with a little giggle, feeling surprisingly like a girl again. "I have to remember to call him Ollie around others. He made me promise."

"You can soothe Sam if it bothers him," Cilla told Abby with a sly grin. "It's not like you can't handle him."

"Ollie is something special to him. He jokes about it being like a mother, but in reality it's more like a father. He didn't like it when he left the ranch, and now it will be permanent."

Rose managed a smile. "You could always move up this way. Might that day come?"

Abby giggled and shook her head. "Over his dead body."

"You know how Ollie feels about Sam. Neither of us had children except those who came into our lives." She looked at Cilla and smiled more widely.

"All right, looks like, surprising though this is, you are old enough to know what you want." Abby reached out and gave Rose's shoulder a squeeze. "After he gets over the shock, Sam will be happy that Ollie is happy."

"Where are you having the wedding?" Grace asked.

"We've been undecided on that." That involved another surprise, but this time it was Ollie's. "I would love it so much if you could all come for it though. He insisted on Valentine's Day as then he'd always remember the right date." She couldn't resist a giggle, but it was nervousness more than anything.

"All right," Cilla said. "We will be here. It gives Cord a month and a half to get the ranch ready to leave. We'll come... all four of us. I promise."

"Of course, Rafe and I will be with Donovan and Danny," Grace added.

Abby sighed. "Of the ranch hands, besides us, who would you like to invite?"

"I know they can't all leave the Rocking R, but he said that he'd especially like it if Joe could come."

"I'll talk to Sam. I am happy for you, Rose. Ollie is dear to us. He's a wonderful man, salt of the earth, strong, and we will be glad he found a woman he could love, once we stop feeling sorry for ourselves at losing him." She rose and gave Rose a big hug.

"Thank you," Rose said. She had overcome that hurdle. Now all she had to do was not feel she was betraying James by remarrying. It wasn't easy. She was happy, but she wished she could have shared this joy with the man who had been all things to her for so many years.

That night, Rose lay in Ollie's arms. Their lovemaking

had again taken her breath away. She kept thinking it would get old or seem stale, but it was always something new, a new way to enjoy her body and now his. Oh how she loved touching his.

"How did Sam feel about it?" she asked as he ran his hand over her breast, teasing a nipple. She had held off asking, as she wanted them to have a relaxing evening. She knew by now that Ollie wasn't a man to talk a lot, but he would tell her whatever she wanted to know.

"Wal," he said with the familiar drawl she had come to love so much. "He didn't believe me at first. Said I couldn't never get a good woman like you to say yes." He laughed.

"He didn't?"

"Yes, he did. I tell ya, that boy is a caution. Anyway, he said he'll stand up with me especially if I need anybody to hold me up. He also said he'd wear a gun."

"For heaven sakes, why?"

"You heard about the second wedding for Abby and him, didn't you?"

"A gun was needed?"

"Sure was, and we all had taken ours off to make it seem more peaceful. Abby didn't much like guns. That day, except for one man having a gun, the parson who had just married them, Sam might've never lived beyond the wedding."

"I do remember that story. I met Pastor Damian once in Tucson. Handsome man, sad eyes, black hair. He was leaving Arizona."

"Yeah, folks don't much take to having a gunman as a pastor, and he was real good with a gun. Surprised the hell out of us—fortunately. Anyway Sam was joking. Ain't nobody wanting revenge on me... or you, I hope." He chuckled.

"No hidden enemies?" she asked as she ran her fingers down his belly to more interesting territory. She liked teasing him and was learning the ways that most led to his responses.

"Not recently." And with that, he bent over her and ended the conversation... the word part anyway.

Christmas morning Rose dressed quickly and hurried downstairs to get the fire started in the kitchen woodstove only to find Ollie had already been there. The kitchen was toasty warm, and he'd even made coffee. She got out bacon and began frying it wondering where he'd gone. A few minutes later she got her answer when he came driving up with a buggy. He tied the horse to the rails.

In the kitchen, he tossed his heavy wool coat over the hook and warmed his hands in front of the stove. "I think it might snow," he said as he accepted a cup of coffee from her.

"Seriously? A white Christmas, who would imagine in Tucson."

"It happens and even more likely out at the Circle C."

"We can use the quilts in the buggy." She began fixing eggs the way he liked them.

"Good idea." They had exchanged their gifts the night before. She had given him a heavy wool scarf, which he was wearing around his neck, as well as a pair of leather gloves. His gift to her had been a turquoise necklace in a Navajo design. The only gift either of them had actually wanted was the love they had found, and it only grew warmer each day. She eagerly awaited the time they could stand in front of their friends and say their vows. Maybe it had been a mistake not to marry immediately, but she knew it hadn't been one to begin sharing a bed. That had reassured her of the rightness of their relationship.

The knock at the door was unexpected. Equally so was the young woman, wrapped in a heavy coat, thin and looking almost ill. Rose ushered her into the kitchen where it was warm. "What can we do for you?" she asked thinking the girl looked strangely familiar, but she was sure she'd never met her.

"I am sorry to disturb you." The woman looked from Rose's face to Ollie's. "I got into Tucson and... I needed to." She stopped, wavering a little. Ollie took her arm and helped her to sit at the table.

"Would you like a cup of coffee or tea?" Rose asked concerned that the young woman might faint.

She shook her head. She looked up then at Ollie. "Are you Roman Alexander Oliver?"

He nodded leaning back against the kitchen counter, one booted foot crossed over the other, as he studied her face. "Do I know you?"

"No, and I don't know you except for your name. You are my grandfather, sir."

Rose looked from the girl up to Ollie's shocked face. "I don't have any children," he said.

"You did not know you had any. My mother told me the story. Mother was born in 1859, Atchison, Kansas."

Rose watched Ollie's face whiten. "And she believed I was her father?"

"Our family holds secrets. She only told me when she

was dying. Her mother had kept the secret until her own death bed. My mother had always been told her father was Frederick Johnson. You knew him, I believe." She coughed into a handkerchief.

"I worked on his ranch, yes."

"My grandmother told my mother that she had not wanted you to know. You were young, didn't have a real job. She felt a child would be better off with her husband as its father. He was a good man, but he died when my mother was a child. My grandmother remarried a good man. Jason Albright. My mother though... she didn't marry my father."

"And your name is?"

Alexa Johnson... I was also not married when my son was born. His father died of an accident a month before Royce came. We had not married because he was already married. We are not a very lucky family, Mr. Oliver."

"This is a lot to take in. Why are you here now?" Ollie asked as he looked over at Rose as though assessing how she was taking this. Not well was the exact truth. She felt stunned, even though Ollie had told her enough of the story for her to believe this was truth.

"For Royce, your great grandson. I am dying, Mr. Oliver. My mother died five years ago. I have no one. My son will have no one when I die. I was hoping you would raise him when I am gone."

Rose sank into a chair. "How do you know you are dying?" she asked finally as worked to steady her voice.

"I've seen doctors. I am not poor, and Royce will not come to you with nothing. I sold the ranch after mother died. I have money to give you to..."

"That's not necessary," Ollie said. "I just haven't had long to get used to this idea."

"What did the doctors say?" Rose asked getting up to make more coffee. It seemed they would need it even if Alexa did not.

"They gave me treatments which they said might help. Arsenic and potassium bicarbonate. It seems it's a disease of the blood. It isn't always responsive. I... I don't have long."

"We have a good doctor here in Tucson," Ollie said his face still showing his working this through. "Where is the boy?"

"We came in on the train. I took a room at the San Xavier. It seemed nice enough and close to the train depot. Royce is six. I got him to take a nap; the train ride had been exhausting, a little frightening for him. The lady who ran the hotel said she would look in on him. I didn't mean to ruin your Christmas. I just wanted to let you know... and have you think about it. I need to get back to my son."

"How would you know I'd be someone you could trust to take care of your son?" Ollie asked.

Alexa smiled for the first time. "I hired a lawyer, Mr. Oliver, who arranged for a detective to find and then investigate you. I was surprised though, when I arrived, to learn you were here in Tucson and not out at the Circle R. I had thought a ranch might be good for raising Royce. Then I got to town, and the lady at the hotel said that Mrs. Redman would know where to find you. The way she smiled made me think... Well, I came here because I wasn't sure how long I really would have to get this worked out for Royce."

"It's a lot to take in," Ollie said his arms now crossed over his chest as he studied the young woman.

"I understand that. I would have waited for spring... but I am not sure I have until spring. I thought if I could be here when Royce met you, it would be easier for him."

"Why don't you go get the boy," Rose suggested, "while I get Alexa settled into the guest room." She looked back at the pale, young woman. "You will be better off here than in the hotel."

"I wouldn't want to impose."

"You won't be. I have a room where you can lie down. You look exhausted."

Alexa managed a smile. Rose looked up then at Ollie. She was unsure how this would impact their marriage or his life, but she knew the first things that had to be done were to care for the boy and his mother. The rest they could work out as they got over the shock.

"What about our family?" he asked but was shrugging into his coat.

"I'll see if this blamed phone works,' she said with a smile that she did not feel. "They will understand."

He shook his head. "Not like I do; why would they?" But he went out the door with no backward look.

CHAPTER 4

Much as Rose hated the use of the phone, there were times it served a purpose. After she got Alexa into bed, she picked up the receiver, cranked the handle and felt relieved to hear Alice come on and agree to ring up the ranch. With the weather as it was, often the call would not go through; so she felt relieved to hear Grace come online.

She waited a moment, to hear Alice hang up her end. More gossip they didn't need, and Alice was quite capable of listening to the calls. When she heard the click, she explained to Grace what had happened.

"My God. What do you want us to do?"

"Just tell everyone that we won't be there."

"Mama will come to you. You know that."

Rose felt relief as she hung up. She needed Cilla. She fought back tears as she considered the sad young woman who had accepted her own death and seemed only to have concern for her son. Then she wondered what impact this would have on her and Ollie.

Within half an hour, he returned with a small, dark-haired boy. "Hello, Royce," Rose said, helping him out of his coat.

"Where is Mama?" he asked looking around the kitchen.

"She's lying down. Would you like to go see her or would you like something to eat?"

"Is she sleeping?"

"She was when I left her."

"Then I'd like something to eat. She has been sick. She needs to rest to get well."

Rose smiled. "I have cookies and can fix you some hot cocoa. How would that be?"

The boy looked around the room again. "I would like that." His manners were impeccable as he sat at the table and waited patiently while Rose set about heating up the chocolate. For a small child, he was very mature. Rose remembered a time, when she had reassured another child, Grace, another forced to make a new life and old for their years.

After James died, Rose had found herself nervous around children but that had been during her time of feeling she was living in a fog. Things had changed. Still was she up to mothering a small child now? She looked over at Ollie who was watching the boy. She had no idea what he was thinking, but he had to be as filled with turmoil as she. They had not expected this level of responsibility, and yet... this was Ollie's flesh and blood. This boy represented the child neither of them had believed they would ever have. Still, she was an old woman. Was she capable of taking on such a charge now?

When she looked up, she saw Ollie studying her.

When he met her gaze, he shrugged and moved to sit at the table across from Royce. "When I picked you up at the hotel, it was not a good time for us to talk with so many strangers around. Do you know who I am?"

"Mama said you would be my great grandfather. Are you?"

"I think so."

"I didn't know my other grandpa."

Rose set the hot cocoa and a plate of sugar cookies in front of him at the same time she heard a wagon stop by the gate. She didn't have to wonder who it would be.

In moments, Sam and Abby Ryker had entered with Cord and Cilla right behind them. They had not brought the children. She felt that was wise although perhaps seeing other children might have reassured Royce.

Sam looked at Ollie. "So you have a grandchild and great grandchild," he said shaking his head. "Ever think about telling me?"

"I would've if I'd have known." Ollie poured each of them a cup of coffee as they settled around the table.

"Alexa is asleep," Rose said. Although she'd told them Ollie's granddaughter was there, she felt compelled to say something. She only wished she had words that would ease the tension. She didn't.

Sam set his hard gaze on the little boy. Rose wondered what was going through his head given his own tumultuous childhood. "How old are you boy?" he asked as he straddled a chair. He and Cord were such big men that she wondered if they would frighten the boy. From the level way he looked from one to the other, it seemed he was not intimidated.

"I will be seven in May." He spoke firmly and with pride.

"You been going to school?" Sam asked.

"Yes sir. I can read and do numbers." He lifted his chin.

Sam looked at Ollie. "Looks like you got a fine great grandson here, Ollie."

"Where is his mother?" Cilla asked turning to Rose.

"Sleeping. She has been sick. She had quite the journey to get here and in the dead of winter."

"I'll just go take a peek in on her if that's all right." Cilla looked back at Royce for permission. When he nodded, she disappeared down the hall. Abby went back out to the wagon and brought in a basket covered with a quilt.

"I nearly forgot this," she said as she put it on the counter. Rose helped her bring out a pie, slices of ham and a scalloped potato dish. "I left the children with Grace and Rafe until we figured this all out," she said, "but we wanted to share our Christmas dinner." She smiled then at Royce. "And it turned out we had something under our tree that Danny and Jesse insisted I bring back in case there was someone here who would like a present."

Royce looked up with interest. "What kind of present?"

"I guess you will have to open it to find out." She reached into the basket and brought out a brightly packaged box tied with red ribbon. She put it on the table in front of the boy.

"For me?"

"It's Christmas, isn't it?" Abby said with a smile.

He pulled on the ribbon and carefully unwrapped the paper. The top of the box lifted off and inside was a die-cast, small train engine with two cars. The engine had big wheels, hooks for the cars, and was painted a bright green. Royce smiled as he moved it across the table and the wheels worked.

Rose felt stunned that the boys, one of the boys had given up such a wonderful toy. It was obvious it had been unwrapped that morning; so the child knew what he was doing. She looked at Abby. "That's a very nice train," she said.

Cilla came back into the room. She smiled as she looked at Royce and then walked to the stove where she poured herself some coffee. Rose and Abby joined her.

"She is very pale and weak. She looks ready to collapse," she said. "I hate to interrupt his Christmas, but I think Cord should go get Doc Hadley. Did she tell you what was wrong?"

"Just that she is dying," Rose said. "Such a tragedy for a young woman like that."

"And she wants Ollie to take Royce," Abby said repeating what they had already been told.

"Yes, it's why she came."

"Either of us could take him," Cilla said. "It would be quite the burden for you and Ollie, just starting your marriage."

Rose glanced over and saw that Ollie was sitting now across from Royce and talking to him quietly. Sam was beside him admiring the new train. She didn't think Ollie was going to be willing to give up this child. Burden or not, the look on his face told her that he would be the grandfather. Would he now though want to go back to the ranch as a better place for the boy to grow up? Was this the end of them?

He looked up at her, but the expression on his face told her nothing.

"I should make some soup, chicken soup," she said as she turned to the counter and began cutting up vegetables. "I had some chicken left over and..." She stopped realizing that she had tears in her eyes. Hiding them from the girls, she set herself to working on what she knew to do—cooking food that would help others get strong, or if need be, to die with ease. She knew about that.

Two days later, Royce had comfortably settled into one of the upstairs bedrooms, visiting his mother when she was awake but amiable to what others wanted. He was an obedient child, but something bothered Rose about him. She could not put her finger on it.

On Doc Hadley's second visit to see Alexa, when he came back to the kitchen, Rose handed him a cup of coffee. George Hadley was a bit younger than her, a fine man, but one who had never married. She had never thought of him as a possible suitor, at least not until the girls asked if he was the man. He wasn't though, fine though he might be.

"Should she be in St. Mary's?" she asked as she sat across from him.

He shook his head. "A hospital won't be better for her. I would only suggest that if her care proves to be too much for you. The doctors who did the tests on her were likely right. There is nothing we can do for her condition."

"It doesn't seem right-- such a young woman."

He shook his head. "Life isn't fair, Rose. You and I both know that all too well."

"Well, she can certainly stay here."

He sipped the coffee. "I will leave you a small bottle of laudanum to use if she should be in pain. A few drops in water will ease her. I doubt it will be that way. I think she will just slip away." He shook his head as he put back on his heavy coat and hat. "I'll try to come by when I can."

Rose had seen people die, too many through her lifetime. She wished she believed it would be otherwise for Alexa. In her heart, she knew the young woman had come to them to find a place for her son. She was now ready to release her hold on life. She wished she had an answer to turn that around, but she didn't. She never had had one for death.

Ollie had not come to her bed since Christmas Eve. They hadn't discussed it, but it had seemed a joint decision. He had moved into the upstairs bedroom across from where Royce was sleeping. Neither of them attempted to talk about their future—if they had one.

Although Cord and Sam had planned to return to their ranches immediately after Christmas, they decided to wait as support for Ollie and Royce. They brought Royce out to the Circle C to meet their children. The boy continued to be surprisingly compliant, and that worried Rose. She was unsure what she could do about it. Did he fully understand the situation with his mother, despite the words he said? His manner reminded her of something, but she could not put her finger on what.

Making more chicken broth, Rose looked up when she saw Ollie ride into the yard. He had told her he would be up to the adobe, the home they had hoped to make theirs. She wondered what he would do with it now. He could not let Royce go to the Circle R without him. It looked as though their future was dying as much as Alexa. She didn't blame the girl or Ollie. It just was what it was. Life was what it was.

She heard his boots on the porch, and felt the same thrill, but now with an ache. They had come so close.

"How is she?" he asked as he came into the kitchen, throwing his coat and hat over the rack before he warmed his hands over the wood stove.

"No better. I am glad Royce is out at the ranch today. I am not sure how much longer she can go on like this. I've tried to get her to eat, but she barely swallows a bite or takes a few sips of water. Doc said she will likely just go to sleep and not wake."

He let out a breath that she hadn't realized he was holding. "I'll go back and sit with her awhile." With that, he was gone. Again, no words about their future or rather lack of one.

On Friday, only four days after she had arrived, Alexa gave a sigh and breathed her last breath. Rose had been sitting with her and saw the moment life departed. Alexa had no last words. Maybe she'd said them all when she first arrived at Rose's home.

Rose sighed and walked back into the kitchen to call Doc and then the Circle C where Royce had been spending the day. She felt he needed to see his mother, to understand what death meant. He was so young. Still, if he didn't see her, wouldn't he always wonder? Cilla said she would bring him there as soon as possible. To give herself something to do with her hands, she made coffee and a fresh pot of tea; then started some cookies.

Half an hour later, seeing Ollie riding into the yard didn't surprise her as much as she supposed it should have since he didn't yet have a phone line to the adobe.

"So she's gone," he said as he came in.

"How did you know?"

His smile was slow. "She came by. Don't ya dare think I've gone nuts."

"No, I understand how that can be. Did she say anything?"

He poured himself coffee. "No, just came by. Maybe another time."

"Do you have visits from the other side often?" She had not thought of him as a psychic like Connie.

"Not often, but it's happened."

"I called Doc. Cilla is bringing Royce back. I thought... he needs to see his mother before... she is buried."

"He's kind of young." He leaned back against the counter as he sipped the coffee and studied her.

She knew then what had been bothering her about Royce. "He's in a fog. Don't you see that? I was in one once. I think he needs to come out of it. A good cry might be a start on that and then his grandpa to hold him in his arms."

He sighed. "All right. I can do the one part, but he'll have to do the other." His smile was faint. The knock at the door ended anything else he might've said.

Doc walked in, headed back to the bedroom and came back to take a cup of coffee. "It was a peaceful end as I thought. You didn't need the laudanum, did you?"

She shook her head. "I was with her. She just sighed once and stopped breathing."

Cilla came driving up with her buggy and Royce. When they were inside, Royce looked from one of them to the other, finally centering on his grandfather. "Is it Mommy?"

Ollie nodded. "Her spirit has left us. Would you like to see her one last time?"

Royce was silent. "I guess so," he said finally, and the two of them went back.

Cilla went to Rose and put her arms around her. "Are you all right?"

"Of course." But she wasn't sure she was.

"You know we would take Royce back to the ranch with us. He's an adorable little boy."

"He's in a bit of a haze right now," Rose said.

"I have seen that."

Doc sat at the table. "It will help that he sees her now. I know it's hard for a small child, but I have seen this before. They need to see the reality, and the natural desire to protect them just makes it harder for them to find new grounding."

Rose pulled the tray of oatmeal cookies from the oven, using a spatula put them on a plate before taking them to the table. She poured him a cup of coffee but kept thinking about the man and boy in the back room. Would seeing his mother's body help Royce break through the fog? Or would it be his grandfather being there for him? Either way she had no part in it.

The three of them sat at the table eating cookies and drinking coffee. Cilla repeated more than once, "I have to stay away from your baking, Rose. I think I gain ten pounds when I come here."

"Well, they look well on you if you do," Doc said with a smile.

"That's what Cord always says... Thank goodness," Cilla said with a little laugh.

When the door opened, Royce came through first. His eyes were red. Ollie was not looking in much better shape. "How about some hot cocoa?" she asked Royce as she had nothing else she could offer. Words weren't likely to comfort him at this moment, and he didn't love her or have any reason to want words from her. Maybe he would even see her as competition for his grandfather's love. She knew she was being silly; Royce was young for such deep thoughts.

The little boy nodded, and she set about heating up milk and measuring out cocoa, grateful for something to do that at least she did well. She heard Doc and Cilla talking, but the words weren't coming through to her. She had to fight to keep the fog away. She was about to lose love again, but she would not let herself sink into depression over it. She had lived before Ollie. She would go on living now.

She realized that he had come to stand behind her. His arms came around her clasping in front. She wanted to lean back against him but was unsure how he meant the gesture.

"I told Royce about the home I been building," he said for her ears only.

"You are thinking of him being there?" she asked. Tears built in her eyes.

"That depends on you."

"Me?"

He moved to where he could see her face. "What do you want, Rose? I know a lot changed this week. It doesn't hardly seem possible it's not even been a week. You weren't counting on all this when you said yes. Have you changed your mind?"

She let the tears fall. "No, have you?"

He smiled then. "Well, I have about one thing."

She felt a chill. "And that is?"

"I want you to marry me right away. I want us to give Royce a home here in Tucson. The home I've been building. I didn't know I'd be needing that extra bedroom for a boy. I'll add on another, as soon as I can, for when family visits. I didn't figure it'd matter, but they were starting up a school out that way. He will need that."

"Yes, he will."

"Rose, will you marry me knowing you will be raising a boy as well as taking on an old cowpoke?"

She tried to stop the sob. It was impossible. She nodded as she wiped away tears. "Yes, I will marry you as soon as we can arrange it."

"Hell." He grinned. "New Year's Eve'll be an easy anniversary to remember too."

"How does Royce feel about it?" He was so young. This was giving him a lot to handle with people he barely knew taking over his life.

"I told him after we talked about his mama and all. He said he'd like having a grandma. He barely knew his. She died when he was a baby. Royce has known a lot of loss for such a young age. He's a smart kid though." He grinned more widely. "He said you make good cocoa."

"Uh oh, the milk."

She turned back to the stove, while wiping away tears. Fortunately it hadn't burned. She stirred in the chocolate and then took it to the table for Royce who was on his second cookie from the looks of the crumbs. He looked up and his gaze met hers. For the first time she saw a clear gaze. The eyes were red-rimmed, but they seemed really to be seeing her. Perhaps fear had been clouding them before.

Cilla looked up at her. "So, what is the plan?"

Rose smiled, feeling some happiness for the first time since Christmas. "Can you stay for a New Year's Eve wedding?"

Doc looked from her to Ollie. "You are getting married?"

"We sure are, and you are invited," Ollie said with a grin. "Then I got to finish up the house as we'll be moving a few miles out of town. I been building us a home on the edge of the Catalinas. It's been nigh finished, just needs a little more work."

"You are a lucky man to have this lady accept you."

Rose was unsure if there was a tone of regret in George's voice. He had never once indicated an interest in her. She could hardly believe he'd had one. Maybe he just wished for a love of his own.

"I shore am," Ollie said. "Nobody knows that more than me and now a grandson to teach about horses and life." He looked at Royce. "You know how to ride, son?"

The boy shook his head, but his eyes looked interested.

Ollie turned to Cilla. "You will all be welcome there as often as you can come. The first time will be for when this lady takes on a broke down old rustler... er rancher. I been fixing a place there for what we figured to be a Valentine's Day wedding, but..." He looked then at Royce. "We got a surprise present for Christmas, and we need to start making our home work for us all."

"I love the idea of a New Year's Eve wedding," Cilla said. "I better get back to the ranch to tell everyone. Then I'll be back to help you get things ready for it, Rose. There isn't much time." With that she was out the door.

CHAPTER 5

Trying to get everything ready for a wedding and helping Royce adjust to his new life, Rose felt she was on the run from first light to last. Of course, being winter, the days were shorter, but they simply weren't long enough.

Her wedding to James had not involved more than a Justice of the Peace. Neither set of parents had approved; so they had to ask someone in the courthouse to stand up with them. She had worn the only good dress she owned, which was a plain gray with a white collar. He had not owned a suit but he had worn his best white shirt. Not having the frills had not mattered. They loved each other, and the days that followed that wedding had involved moving a lot for a time and then settling in Tucson to keep house for the Wesleys and become second parents to Priscilla.

This wedding, with so many more friends, was to be very different. She didn't intend to invite her bridge friends, but she would want the Cordovas there and that entailed a lot of people and children. She sent word to Maria and was told, of course, they'd all be delighted to attend. Naturally, Maria also offered to help with food. She was such a wonderful friend.

On Saturday, when she went to personally tell Connie the wedding date was moved up, her friend had smiled broadly. "A very auspicious time to marry. You will be at the beginning of a new century. With December 31st, you will be saying good-bye to the old and hello to the new. Would you like me to do a reading to double check it?"

Rose smiled. She didn't doubt Connie's gift, but she had confidence in the future with Ollie. She didn't need a reading. She shook her head. "Like I could tell Ollie that we can't marry on Monday because it's not okay with the stars." She could just imagine his response.

Connie laughed. "Good point. Then I get to provide the wedding gown. I had ordered it and luckily it got here early." She went to the closet and brought out a cloth covered hanger. She lifted the cloth to reveal a gown of a soft off white. Lace at the cuffs and neck softened the simple lines as did the bodice with lace in a V down its front.

"It's gorgeous," Rose said at a loss for words. "It has to be too expensive."

"You don't measure cost when it's a gift. I saw it in a catalog and knew it was for you. I didn't expect it to come early with Christmas and all. I guess someone in the fates knew better than me. You must wear it."

Rose smiled with tears again rolling down her cheek. "I will and thank you so much."

"All you need is something for your hair." Connie

went to the store and came back with a length of chantilly lace. "This will be perfect."

"You shouldn't do all this."

"Of course, I should. Neither you nor I had a real wedding the first time. I will be happy to see you have one this time. Ollie is a good man; and now with Royce, you two have your own family." They sat at the table to drink some of Connie's special tea.

"Royce is an amazing boy," Rose said. "I do see Ollie in him, and I think it's why they have bonded so quickly. They both went up to the house today as they have been doing whatever is needed to get the house ready for guests."

"Where is it?"

"Out of town, a bit east of Pima Canyon. A small stream flows through it most of the year. He built the house though high enough to avoid mountain flashfloods."

"Does it worry you being out so far out?"

"If I lived alone, maybe. I like the idea of having the desert around me and learning more about it. I have lived in Tucson since 1871 and know almost nothing about the desert. Ollie knows those things. He said he could teach Royce. I want to learn also."

Connie smiled. "It will be beautiful. I get tired of being in towns also. The Apaches at least won't be a problem, but there still are brigands who roam the backcountry."

"From what I know, Ollie is good with a gun. He usually wears one when he's been heading up there. It was another thing he was going to teach Royce about, as he didn't want there to be an accident with him not understanding guns. I guess he'll have to be a little more careful where he stores his now."

"Del also is good with a gun. He's had to use it a few times when someone... well has gotten angry at my gift... or back when he was gambling. Poor losers." She managed another smile.

"I have never fired one, but now... well, I should learn also. I am eager to learn new things. I can hardly believe that, at almost 61, I could be embarking on something new. It's almost too good to be true." She pinched herself.

"It's good. I see that and don't need to do a reading. It is sad that Holly will miss the wedding. I know she hoped to be back by late January, but this probably is out of the question."

"I felt bad about that also. I telegraphed her, of course, but there is no way she could be here in time. We can't wait now that Royce is a factor. The boy needs stability, a home he can rely on. It makes no sense to put off the wedding." And she was tired of a lonely bed at night. She wanted him back in her arms when the lights went out. And besides, until they actually were married, she would feel insecure that something would come between them.

"How soon will you be moving out there?"

They had not discussed that. "I am not sure. He's been vague lately about how much progress he's been making. I do know that Cord, Sam, Rafe, and David were helping today—maybe Raul. Although with Royce along, that may delay things."

"My goodness. How old is David now? Children grow up so fast."

"He is fifteen and nearly a head taller than Abby. He looks like he's heading for his father's height or more."

"It is my one life regret that Del and I could not have children."

"I had felt I had one with Cilla even though she's mine by love not blood."

"We moved around so much that I didn't even have that. I guess I made my own choices, and I do adore Del; so..." She sipped her tea. "What will you do with your house?"

"Although she gave it to me, it belongs to Cilla. She has paid the costs of it and has in addition given me a generous stipend for the years I worked for her. I do own some of the furniture, which likely will go to our new home. I want to transplant some of my roses too. Ollie brought river soil up there for a garden."

"I'm happy for you my friend. I haven't seen you looking so beautiful or even young in all the years I have known you."

Rose blushed but wasn't willing to tell Connie that's what good sex had done for her. She wasn't embarrassed that she and Ollie had already been lovers, but she also wasn't prone to discussing intimate details, even with a dear friend. Besides, she'd barely had a kiss from him since Christmas. Maybe it was anticipation that could account for the changes her friend saw.

"Let me know where to bring the dress, and I'll take care of that," Connie said as she walked Rose to the street.

Rose hugged her before she left to start walking up Congress toward her home.

"Hey you," a female voice yelled.

Rose turned and laughed as she saw the tall blonde. Even having had Holly living with her for months, her beauty still took Rose's breath away. She was as beautiful as any woman Rose had ever seen. More than that, she had both an innocence and toughness to her lovely features that made her face constantly interesting and changing.

"How did you manage to get here?" she asked as Holly pulled her into her embrace.

"It was an emergency, of course. I was not going to let you marry that man."

"What?"

Holly giggled. "Without me there. My gosh, Rose, I thought you'd never realize what he wanted and that he was the one. He's so sexy. It's lucky for you that I want to remain unmarried, or I'd have gone after him myself." She laughed again.

"Then it's good you wish to be a spinster," Rose said with a pretend huff, "as I'd hate for us to be fighting over a man."

"Well, he'd probably think I was too young for him anyway. I doubt he ever looked my way or at any other woman. He knew what he wanted, and he's the kind of man to go after it. I just had to be there when you two get this signed sealed delivered."

"I can't believe this. How did you get here so fast?"

"I'd like to tease you longer, but... I was on my way back. The telegraph was forwarded to me only when I touched down here. I had been able to conclude my business in Chicago right before Christmas. I needed to get out of there and back to the desert."

It was Rose's turn to laugh. "Well, however it happened, I am so glad you will be here. Have you already seen Clint?"

"Why would I want to see him before you?"

"All right, be that way," Rose said, with a little snort. "Then tell me how did it go with your father's estate?"

Holly sighed as they began to walk. "I will tell you... like after you're married and settled. I really don't want to talk about it. My sister was... Well, just let's say she is the bitc—the brat she's always been. The main thing is the business is concluded, and I am back in Arizona and free. I won't have to go back." She made a sound of disgust.

"Then good for us. Where are your bags?"

"As soon as I read the wire, I arranged for a room at the Orndorff. I expected you would have a full house."

"I always would have room for you."

"I know but... Amazing news that Ollie has a great grandson."

"It has been shocking. We are burying Royce's mother Sunday and marrying Monday evening. Death and a wedding together."

"Life can be a little that way. Always the surprises." At the tone in Holly's voice, Rose turned to look at her. There was sadness in those beautiful eyes. "Hey, it'll be better now that I am back," the younger woman said and smiled.

At Rose's gate, she stopped to look at her roses trying to decide, which she might safely move. It was a good season for that at least. To raise roses in the desert, even the hearty climbers, required careful nurturing, watching for where they would not get too much sun, being sure they had enough water but not too much. Gardening had been one of her joys. She would turn it toward more vegetables with a man and growing boy to feed, and their home farther from the markets.

In the house, they took off their coats, and she started tea water. "Are you sure you don't want to stay here?"

Holly shook her head. "Not now." She looked around the kitchen. "I do like this house. Will you and Ollie live here?"

"No, that's part of the news I couldn't share in a wire. He has been building us a home out of town."

"What about this one?"

"It actually belongs to Cilla." She opened the tea tin for a blend she knew Holly liked.

"It's centrally located. I wonder if Cilla would sell it."

"I don't know."

"I would rent it if she wants to hold onto it. It'd be perfect for the times when I am in town."

"You make it sound as though that might not be a lot." She poured the hot water over their tea.

"You know I had been hoping to get back for a dig in the Cibicue country. I can afford to fund that now."

"You talked of that before. Didn't Ollie tell you that region is not safe? I know the feud is finished, the Apaches no longer raiding, but... I mean couldn't you explore closer to Tucson. I've been told the Romero Ranch has ruins on it. I would hazard a guess that they'd be happy to let you explore there."

Holly got an expression on her face that Rose had seen before. "Let's not discuss this. I want to help you with your wedding. Where are you going on your honeymoon?"

"I don't see how we could go anywhere, with Royce to be considered."

Holly's expression was contemplative. "I suppose Cilla and Abby will be going home right after the wedding."

"They've already been away longer than they had planned."

"I guess he'd be a bit much for Grace, with Danny and a new baby."

"I wouldn't ask her. She's a natural mother, but she's also had everyone out there for the holidays."

"Well, I will talk to Cilla about the house, and you need a honeymoon. I will take care of Royce, while you two take a few days for yourselves."

"You are comfortable with small children?" That didn't fit the image Rose had of the beautiful woman who had been born with the silver spoon and servants to take care of everything. What could she know about a small boy?

"Oh well, there is that." Holly laughed. "All right. Plan B. I will stay out at the ranch with Grace while you two go off. I'd like time to visit her anyway. We can ask, can't we?"

"Ollie might not want to..."

"Want to what?" he asked as he and Royce came through the door. For once Rose hadn't heard his arrival. "Hey, pretty lady, how'd you get back here so fast?" he asked with a big grin.

Holly jumped to her feet and ran into his welcoming arms. "I was already heading south. Who wants to be in

Chicago in the winter when they can be in Tucson?" She laughed as she then turned to look at Royce. "And this is your great grandson. He looks a lot like you, Mr. Oliver."

Royce looked at her with curiosity, as Ollie threw their coats over the rack and grabbed Rose in a bear hug that all but crushed her bones. Well, not really, but it was satisfyingly close and what she had been wanting all day.

"How was your day, wife to be?"

"I visited with Connie before I came across Holly on her way out here. Were the boys helpful on the house?"

"They were still up there with Raul, when I left. Royce was getting tired. And yes, we made a lot of progress. It's ready for us to not only get married there but live, that is if you are willing to do without all that you have here."

"Does it have a stove?"

He nodded. "But wood for now. No ice box yet either, but I am pushing for the wires to reach there within the month. We should have a phone by then too. I am not the only one who saw the beauty of living in that region. The acres below ours have been sold and two homes are going up."

"Good thing you got ten acres then," Rose said as she heated up coffee for him. "And I could manage with wood again. I like cooking that way—until summer comes anyway."

"Actually I bought forty when the price was good. Figured just in case this happened, I wanted not to have neighbors right on my door. Besides I needed it for the big barn and corrals."

"You need a big barn?"

"For the horses. I was thinking of doing some training there. The kind that doesn't get a man tossed, but where he convinces the horse to do what he wants by talking the animal into it."

"You can do that?" Rose asked with some surprise. Then again, she remembered how he whispered to her. Smiling reminiscently, she had no doubt he could convince a horse to bend to his will.

"I can. And now that we have Royce." He looked at the boy with another smile. 'I figured we also need a dog."

"Really, we can have a dog?" Royce asked with big eyes.

"Have to have one. Good dog makes a home a home." He looked back then at Rose. "Unless you don't want one."

She smiled. Like she could say no now. "Actually, I'd like a dog too," she said. "This project though is growing like topsy."

"He laughed again. "Maybe so. I guess I have been rushing you since you first said yes."

"Nothing I haven't wanted also, Mr. Oliver," she said with that familiar feeling of warmth flooding through her.

"You will love it up there. The house will be the coolest you've ever lived in, with the thick adobe walls and the overhanging verandas. Wait 'til you spend a summer there. You won't ever want to live with wood again."

"What are the floors like?" Holly asked with interest as she went to the cupboard and found the cookie jar for Royce.

"Tile and I have waxed them with three coats," Ollie said with pride in his voice. "You know I never had a home of my own. Saved a lot of money that way and now I know why I was needing it." He grinned.

"Where are you taking Rose for a honeymoon?" Holly asked with her usual directness.

For once Ollie looked flummoxed. "I hadn't thought of that. There is Royce."

"We worked that out," Holly said. "Royce and I will go out and stay with Grace a few days and help her with the baby. Royce will like time with Danny, I bet." She looked down at the boy.

"I like Danny," he said as he took another cookie.

"It would only be a few days."

Rose smiled. She remembered how Holly had been the first time she met her, a little uncertain. Whether it was going to Chicago and settling her father's affairs or just her natural self blossoming, she wasn't uncertain now.

"And on the horses," Holly said, "actually I took some riding lessons when I was in college. I need to get better at handling them if I want to go up to the Cibicue. I could use some more though if you considered giving lessons with your enterprise."

Ollie frowned. "I don't mind teaching you about horses, gal, but I told you the Cibicue is not a good idea. That's rough country. Did you talk to Clint or Gabe about this?"

Rose recognized that stubborn look that came over Holly's face. "I don't need anybody's permission for it— certainly not theirs."

"Well Raul, Gabe's papa, he knows a lot about that region. You need to know a hell of a lot more than you do right now-- if you are going to spend time up there. It's not just rugged country but often has some men who would consider you just a tempting morsel." His smile was crooked.

Holly answered his smile with a teasing look of her own, which Rose knew won over most men. "I can do that... but it won't change my mind, Mr. Oliver."

Ollie shook his head. "Gotcha. Still knowing what is there is better than riding in blind. And it would take you several months to get good enough at horses if all you had were eastern riding lessons." He grimaced. "Riding in circles or on groomed paths ain't what you will find up in the Cibicue. It's real pretty country, but... You need to talk to Rafe and Raul."

"I hear you," she said with a frown. "Can we discuss the wedding or better yet the honeymoon?" She smiled when he did.

"I need to think some on the honeymoon idea." He looked back at Rose who had poured milk for Royce. "But it's growin' on me," he drawled with that Kansas twang he could use when he chose. His smile had Holly laughing.

The funeral service Sunday afternoon for Alexa Oliver Johnson was simple with only close friends of Ollie and Rose attending. When it was explained to him what it entailed, Royce said he would like to come. The other children stayed with Grace and Rafe at the ranch, as it was a cold day, looked again like snow might be possible.

For the burial at the Court Street Cemetery, Abby took Royce back to the ranch. Brave little boy though he had been, seeing his mother's body put into the ground seemed a bit much for a child.

As the eight of them walked away from the graveyard, Rose put her arm around Ollie. She saw the sadness on his face and wished she had words to make it better.

"You okay, old man?" Sam asked from his other side.

"Will be. Just wish I'd been told about her mama and had a chance to know Alexa. Now I never will."

"You have a chance now with Royce. Just be glad for that. He looks like a fine young boy, brave as hell," Sam said. "David really likes him, says though to watch out as he's a risk taker." Sam grinned. "He'll be a handful for you in another few years."

Rose glanced over at Connie, who was now walking at her other side. She knew that despite the possibility Connie could connect with Alexa or her mother, Ollie was unlikely to want that. She remembered then how he had felt Alexa pass by as she left life. Perhaps the girl would come back to him and give him reassurances.

She wished she knew more about how that all worked. In the past, being a woman of simple interests, she hadn't cared a lot. She believed in Connie's gift, encouraged others to seek her help. For herself, she only would ask for a reading if Ollie requested it.

As she looked up at him, she saw by the set of his jaw, he'd not be asking.

"I hope you will come to the house for a bite to eat," she said to Del and Connie as they came to what would have been a parting of their ways.

"Not today," Connie said. "But we will see you tomorrow." She smiled then and gave Rose a quick embrace before they headed for their store.

CHAPTER 6

At the house, Cord reached for the whiskey and poured a shot for each man while Cilla started tea.

"Will Joe or Rock make it in for the wedding?" Ollie asked Sam as he sipped his whiskey.

"I tried to get word to them. We still don't have a phone line; so it all depends on whether someone goes in for supplies. Offhand, my guess is they won't."

"Would've been nice to see them there, but I understand. Maybe we can throw a party later in the spring and get everybody."

Rose came to sit beside her soon-to-be husband. "I would like that. You have been a little reluctant to share the arrangements for tomorrow." She gave his shoulder a little punch.

"Wal, I figured I'd grab you and carry you off. Then..."

She punched him a little harder.

"If she going to brutalize you like that," Sam said with a laugh, "maybe you better think twice on this wedding."

"I'd like to hear the plans also," Cilla said as she and Cord sat at the table. "Holly mentioned a honeymoon."

"I did," Holly said as she sat beside Cord. "They should have a few days without being parents and just for them. Maybe stay in one of the hotels and dance at Carrillo Gardens."

"That isn't my thing at all," Rose said. "But this idea of a few days, just us, I like that one. So yes, let's have Royce stay out at the Circle C, if Rafe and Grace agree."

"I already called them about it," Holly said. "They said fine. I'll go out right after the wedding. Well, I guess most of us will."

"Do you want all the children there? And who is marrying you?" Cilla asked.

"Judge Amory is doing the deed," Ollie said. "We got the license as soon as she said yes. And it will be at the adobe. Our home. I have it ready for it."

"What time?" Sam asked.

"You come up earlier since you will be standing up with me," Ollie said.

"God," Sam said with a teasing note, "likely be holding you up."

Ollie chuckled. "Not going to be needed." He looked at Rose with that smile that had her heart melting.

"So Cilla and I will come up at what time?" Holly asked.

"Leave here at five. I want you up there just as the sun starts to set," Ollie said.

"My God," Sam said with a laugh. "You are a sentimental galoot. Marry her New Year's Eve and at sunset. Who knew?"

Cord refilled their glasses. "Not you for sure. Not like you are the romantic type."

"I can be," Sam said defensively and then laughed again. "There are moments."

Cilla gave Cord's shoulder a slap. "The pot calling the kettle black?"

Both brothers laughed. "Okay, okay. We will learn maybe from the master here." They raised their glasses to Ollie.

"Hey, I had a lot of time to think about this," Ollie said. "Wasn't sure she'd ever say yes. I do have some ideas, but ain't like I am a total romantic either." He gave them both one of his looks, which had the two younger men chuckling again.

Ollie rose then. I better go get Royce. He and I are sleeping up there tonight. I named it by the way. At least unless Rose here has a different idea."

"I'd like to hear it before I decide that," she said smiling.

"I should whisper it to you," he said giving Cord and Sam another look. "Not like I want to hear them make fun of me again."

"You being such a weak soul and all," Sam retorted.

"All right, all right, so I don't give a damn what you think. I been calling it Casa de Amor."

The two younger men burst out laughing again, but Rose and Cilla smiled broadly. "You could learn from him," Cilla told Cord. "I love that name. It's what it will be too. I know it."

Ollie walked to the door but waited for Rose to join him. "On the porch," he said and took her hand to draw her out, ignoring the renewed laughter from the kitchen.

"I won't see you until you walk up the path to our home," he said. "You know what luminarias are, don't you?"

She nodded.

"The torches will light your way. And at the top, I built us a ramada, using ocotillo and saguaro ribs. We can use it a lot of ways later, but tomorrow, it will be where I'll be waiting."

"I love that idea and at sunset." Her smile softened, and she felt that familiar glow spread through her body. "Should I bring up food for afterward?"

"I'll have that too. I arranged for Carrillo's to bring up a spread. I don't want you to have to do anything tomorrow except walk up that path to me." He bent then and tenderly kissed her lips. "Until tomorrow, soon-to-be Mrs. Oliver."

She felt tears again. "I will be there, Mr. Oliver."

"I'll get us some reservations at the Xavier if you'd like that."

"I'd rather somewhere else if that's all right with you."

"Whatever you want. Where?"

"Let's start our marriage in our new home... I hope it has a bed, but if not, well, we can sleep on the floor. I want to have time there with just you before we have Royce, and we are a family."

He grabbed her into his arms again, and this time his tongue delved into her mouth with his kiss. "There is a bed," he said when he finally came up for air. "And yes, Holly and Cilla can take Royce back with them to the ranch after we have the wedding supper."

She was almost shaky when she walked back inside to hear the whistles from Sam and Cord. "Looks like House of Love will earn its name," Sam said with a laugh. "If

Ollie's been my mama, does that make you my papa?" He smiled and stood to pull her to him for a hug.

"Maybe we can both be the mama," she said when he released her.

"Sounds like a plan to me."

"God, I got to get Cilla out of here before she starts wanting sweet nothings from me," Cord teased.

"It's too late for that," she said, but she threw her arms around her husband. "Although, I haven't any complaints actually." She kissed his neck. "We though do need to get back to the ranch, help Grace with the evening meal, and get the children lined up for how they will behave tomorrow. The last wedding Jesse attended, he was less than respectful."

"He's just a boy," Rose said.

"But a boy with too much enjoyment of joking. All right, we are off. I will be back here about noon tomorrow, Rose."

When they had all gone except Holly, Rose was relieved at the quiet that fell over the house.

"Did you talk to Cilla about the house?" she asked Holly.

"Yes, and she said we can work it out. I'll want my own furniture. I had actually arranged to have some shipped to Tucson before I left Chicago. Most of this can either be taken by you or sold, I guess."

Rose went to the cupboard. "Would you like some red wine?" she asked as she brought out the bottle.

"I would love it. And a toast." When she had her glass, Holly lifted it. "To two of the nicest people I know. I may not have a chance to do a toast tomorrow. It seems it's usually the task of the gentlemen, but i just want you to know how much you have meant to my life and then Ollie."

When they had taken several sips, Rose said, "And you to mine. I was in a bit of a daze until Grace came back and then you. You were such a gift to me with how you brought life into this house. I am glad you will be the one living in it next."

"Me too. How about a second glass of wine?"

Rose laughed and poured them each another. She didn't need the wine though to feel the glow. Just the anticipation of the next day was enough for that.

With the knock on the door, Holly groaned when she saw who was standing on the porch. "I had hoped he wouldn't show up so soon."

"I thought you liked Clint," Rose said.

"As a friend."

"Well then, just be sure you let him know that."

"I have. Maybe I am making too much of him showing up now."

The almost too handsome lawyer walked into the kitchen, removing his hat to reveal neatly trimmed blond hair. "I heard about the wedding," he said, looking at Rose before he looked at Holly with an expression of surprise. "I didn't realize you were back. How are you?"

"I am well."

"You are, of course, invited to come," Rose said. "It will be at Ollie's home, well, mine now too. We will be leaving here at five. You can follow us up if you like."

"I'd like that." He looked back at Holly. "You finished your business in Chicago?"

"Enough to leave," she said. "I would have gotten in touch with you, Clint. I wanted to tell you in person. I have arranged for James Angus to be my attorney here in Tucson. My lawyers in Chicago recommended him highly, and it made it easier for them to transfer papers."

Clint tightened his lips. "Angus is a good man. No problem. Whatever works for you. Can we have dinner soon?"

"I will be busy for awhile. I will let you know if I get some time." She hadn't said any of it in a friendly tone.

"I would like that."

"Would you like a glass of wine, Clint?" Rose asked trying to soften the atmosphere in the room.

"No thanks. I will though come to the wedding. I'll follow you up as you suggested. Thank you." He picked up his hat and was out the door without a backward glance or a goodbye.

"I suppose i made him angry," Holly said. "I can't help it. He wanted something I did not. To be honest, much as I am happy for you and Ollie, I don't ever want to be married."

"Why?"

Holly sipped her wine. "One good reason is I don't want to ever lose control of my life again. Women can run their own affairs up until they get married; then the husband takes over."

"I thought laws had been changed regarding that."

"Law or not, the men take over. I've seen it. My mother had the money in their marriage. She lost all control over it. She died a broken woman because of the cruelty of my father, and she had no recourse to escape."

"I am sorry to hear that but not all men are like that."

"A man like Ollie, Cord, Rafe, or even Sam, maybe not. There aren't many out there like that."

"How about Rafe's brother, Gabriel? You know he's likely to be there tomorrow with all the Cordovas."

"Stop being a matchmaker," Holly said with a smile and little giggle. "I just want to be happy for you. I have other plans for myself."

"Doing an archaeological dig up on the Cibecue. I wish you'd reconsider that."

Holly smiled again. "All right. Let's just forget I said it. I have plenty to do to make your home into mi casa."

"All right. I should go to bed. The wine has made me sleepy, and tomorrow I have a lot to do. Connie will be here also just after lunch with my dress. We will have a real hen party." She giggled and knew the wine was having an effect.

"All right. I'll just clean the kitchen. You go onto bed. I'll lock up when I leave."

"Bring your bags when you come tomorrow; so it'll be easier to go out to the ranch after the wedding."

"Good idea." Holly gave her a hug. "I do believe in love, Rose. I have seen it. So don't feel sorry for me, or even think I am a hopeless case. Just there are other things that are important for a woman. We have that choice now."

"All right. I won't nag you on it." With that Rose went to bed. She lay there for nearly an hour as she thought about the step she would be taking. She felt no doubts. This was everything she wanted. She would not be sleeping alone again. Royce would make their home into more of a real one. She felt excited at the prospect of all that lay ahead.

After an enjoyable day with her friends, lots of laughter and teasing, finally it was time for Rose to slide into the dress Connie had brought for her. When she adjusted the lace scarf over her head, in the mirror, she did look like a bride.

"You are beautiful," the women said in unison. Grace, with Donovan in her arms, kissed her cheek. "I am so happy for you," she added.

The buggy ride, which, with four buggies, was a bit of a procession, seemed to pass in an instant. Del drew their buggy to a halt at the bottom of a little rise. She could see the line of torches, the path and at the top, the promised ramada. More importantly, she could see Ollie standing there, wearing the first dark jacket she had ever seen on him with a white shirt and string tie.

Sam walked down to her and took her arm. "I get the honor," he said. They waited at the bottom until Grace, Abby, and Connie had walked up to join the Cordovas and other guests. Cilla followed them. From somewhere Ollie had found a violinist, and the familiar wedding march sounded out across the desert. As she walked up the path, she was glad for Sam's strong arm to be sure she didn't stumble. Her knees were trembling.

Finally, she was beside Ollie. He took her hand. They turned to face the judge who began saying the words. She was barely aware of what they were, but she repeated words when requested. It was only when Ollie turned to Royce for the ring that she realized there was one. He slid the gold band onto her finger, and then the Judge pronounced them man and wife. She was crying again.

He tipped her head up and kissed her lips. She supposed he intended it to be a light kiss, but she threw her arms around his neck and pulled him tightly to her, for the first time pushing his lips apart with her tongue. Despite his surprise, he quickly met her kiss with equal fervor, and there were long moments before they broke apart.

"By God," Sam said with a laugh, "damned good they got married is all I can say." The guests all laughed as each took their turns kissing and hugging the couple.

When Rose looked to the west, it was to see a striking sunset. The sky was crimson with clouds of all shapes offering various levels of color. "You ordered that too," I suppose," she said as Ollie took her in another embrace and they watched the majesty of one of Arizona's finest.

When it finally began to diminish, Ollie said, "Please, all of you come on inside and join us for our first meal as husband and wife." He grinned then and added, "Just don't stay too long." Sam and Cord laughed and slapped him on the back as they all went into the house.

Rose had seen the home, but he had made wonderful progress since her last visit. She loved the kitchen with a long table, which would seat almost all their guests. There were flowers on the counters. As Ollie had promised, a virtual feast had been provided by Carrillos. She walked to the woodstove, and then approved the view out the window behind the sink.

"We'll get it better as we can," Ollie said as he came up behind her.

"It's perfect now. I am going to love living here." She turned and gave him a light kiss. "Just a sample of what is coming," she whispered.

"We better eat then. I'll need my strength," he teased.

They joined the others, laughed and talked. She

heard little of it because her heart was so full of his near-ness, of the promise of all that was to be.

Finally Sam said, "Time for us to go before this old rustler chases us out." He laughed.

"Can we stop by and pick up my bag at Rose's?" Holly asked. "I packed just what I'll need at the Circle C."

Royce looked worriedly at Ollie. "You... sure I can't stay here with you tonight? I liked it last night."

"What and miss all the fun out at the ranch," Holly said giving him a hug. "I have something special for you and the other children... even you, David." She looked at the fifteen year old and winked. "Christmas presents, of course that I wasn't here to give you earlier."

"One for me too?" Royce asked now with interest.

"Absolutely. So let's hurry out to the ranch. We need to have a little time before bed for you all to unwrap your gifts and maybe play a little before you're too sleepy."

Royce looked back at his grandfather. "Just one night?"

"Two and then I'll come get you," he said as he hugged the boy. "You be good until then... Well even after then. We will be living up here all the time. You'll be sleeping in your own room like you did last night."

The boy considered that but then nodded.

Less than an hour later, Ollie and Rose were finally alone. "Are you going to show me our bedroom?" she asked. "I haven't seen it with furniture."

"Of course, I even bought you a little something for it." He led her back to the room she knew was to be theirs. In the center of one wall was a large bed with a beautiful pine frame. A long dresser took up another wall and a tall wardrobe was on the third. On the wall, with a window, a door led out to the back of the property.

"It's beautiful. So much to take in."

"And one more gift."

"I'd love that."

"Well," he said with a sly smile. "This one might be more for me than you. It's in the dresser. I'll be back in a few minutes."

"You don't need to leave. I will need help getting out of this dress."

His smile broadened. "I couldn't leave you with that problem, now could I?"

"No, and I will need to help you, of course."

"I like the sound of that."

Hours later, they woke, the lacy nightgown had been discarded, but she made sure it wasn't torn in the process as she planned to wear it again. She ran her hands lightly over his muscular chest. "I see that married sex is as good as unmarried," she teased.

"Mrs. Oliver, I plan to make it better and better the longer we are married."

"Well, of course. I knew that."

"The ramada would be a good place for us to uh... have a meaningful discussion." He blew a breath against her temple.

"And the kitchen."

"The parlor. No furniture in there yet but there is a kiva fireplace and several quilts should do it."

"Wonderful. And Roman..."

"Yes."

"Let's not make Royce wait to come home. I think if we got him late this afternoon, he'd be happier and know we really wanted him."

She felt his smile against her skin. "Rose Redman Oliver, I do love you. I love you for the woman you are but also the love you bring to everyone around you. Yes, we should do that because by then, you'll be so tired of making love to me, you'll be glad to have a rest."

She giggled and ran her fingers down his belly. "Oh I expect we will continue making love... just have to be a little more discrete is all. Little boys sleep pretty soundly if they play hard all day... not to mention when he's at school."

"All right then... We will start the first day of the new year as a family."

"And Roman..."

"Yes."

"You are my gift. All the gift I will ever want."

The End

This theme continues with Echoes From The Past, A Taggert family introduction. Sample attached.

ECHOES FROM THE PAST

A Taggert novel by Rain Trueax.

INTRODUCTION

They had absolutely no reason to be together-- nothing in common-- except, oh maybe a few past lives where the passion was sizzling—with a minor complication—he always ended up dead. Pure coincidence. Couldn't happen again. Her fear that it could led her to try to convince him not to go with her on a potentially dangerous archaeological investigation to Central Arizona, where one of those lives had been haunting her dreams.

He knew, given his experiences, there were many ways he could end up dead, and he wasn't about to worry about dreams with no real bullets. He did know, however, that she could prove dangerous to him. He had never walked away from danger before and wasn't about to now.

1901, a new century and things should be less wild and woolly in Arizona. Very civilized, with only an occasional nightly shootout. Much safer—for some. Not so much for the son of an infamous outlaw family, who was falling in love with the one woman from whom he should have stayed many miles away. Shoulds weren't in his vocabulary.

This western adventure takes these two unlikely lovers from Tucson, north into the Sierra Ancha, where answers and danger await. As the fifth Arizona historical, readers of the others will find some familiar characters.

This is the first romance for the Taggert brothers-- Vince, Jesse and Cole.

PART I
CHAPTER 1

April 1901, Tucson, Arizona

Holly Jacobs looked at the mare Señor Perez had led from the stall. The hostler frowned as he studied her face. "You look frightened, señorita. Horse know this." She had hoped she was hiding her fear. "No, I am fine." She was lying, did not like lying and sucked in a breath.

Princess, a four-year old mare, had been purchased with the recommendation she was a reliable mount. She looked good. Light brown, strongly muscled, neither sway-backed, nor with damaged hocks, she was told she would make a good mount. Her mistake might have been to trust Clint Madison with finding a horse for her. One, she didn't want to owe him a favor. Two—what did he know about horses. He might be a good enough lawyer but that meant little where it came to evaluating a horse.

She should have asked Ollie Oliver's opinion, but he had been so busy. No, this would be fine for her first time on the mare—hopefully, since it also was her first time with the new sidesaddle.

Taking lessons from Ollie, she had developed a reasonable amount of confidence while riding on the trails around his ranch. He though had always insisted that ladylike concerns were... Well the phrase he used wasn't one she was comfortable remembering. The long and short of it was-- ride astride until she had control of herself and the horse. Ollie had provided her with boys' britches and insisted she take her lessons astride. That was hardly proper when she was in Tucson. She could manage a sidesaddle. Ladies rode that way wearing proper riding skirts. How difficult could it be?

She stepped up on the block and situated herself on the saddle. Arranging her knee properly over the fixed head, her other leg under the leaping head, it felt right. This was going to be fine. She straightened her skirts before smiling and reaching for the reins from Señor Perez.

"You want I go with you?" he asked with that uneasy voice.

"That won't be necessary but gracias." She lightly touched her riding crop to Princess's rump, and the horse stepped out of the barn.

It had been several years, but she had ridden sidesaddle in the east. Never that far and never alone. She wanted this to be alone, to prove to herself that she could do it. If she couldn't do it, how could she get to her archaeological exploration on the Cibecue? She had to do it.

The roads leading from Tucson were full of other horsemen, people walking with burros, and heavily laden wagons. Past one home, small children jumped up and down laughing. No one paid her notice as she passed. With the smooth gait of Princess, her confidence grew.

She would take Princess out of town but not as far as Oracle. They didn't need a long ride. This was to put herself at ease and let her horse grow familiar with her. She smoothed her hand over the mare's neck. "We'll do fine, won't we," she said-- whether to reassure herself or the horse, she wasn't sure.

April was a delight on the desert with fields of colorful wildflowers. Even a prickly pear was coming into bloom. The breeze was faint, a lovely day for a ride with a sky full of fluffy clouds, passing in no hurry. She turned her mare to the north road and the traffic thinned out. Toward the mountains would be Ollie's ranch, but she wouldn't ride that far. Perhaps she'd take the sidesaddle and Princess to him for her next lesson. Rose, Ollie's wife, would enjoy seeing her riding like a lady.

After having ridden what she judged was about four miles beyond the outskirts of Tucson, she pulled on the left rein and turned Princess back toward the stable. It was then that the mare took it into her head to run. Trying to resist shrieking, which wouldn't be effective in stopping her, she pulled on the reins, but Princess had it in her head where she was going. The tightening bit wasn't changing her mind.

Holly's fear rose as she struggled to stay in the saddle. What would happen when they reached all those wagons, the burros, would Princess slow then? If she did, could Holly keep on her when she already felt unbalanced.

It was then that she heard the thunder of hooves, and a horse came alongside, the rider a stranger in dark garb. "You all right, ma'am" he yelled as he pulled his mount to match her horse's running gait.

"Do I look all right?" she yelled. She let out a shriek as he reached out a long arm and in seconds had pulled her from her saddle and had her in front of his. She felt even more frightened than she had when about to fall off her running horse.

He slowed his mount to a stop, gave her a cursory look, one that saw but didn't at the same time. "I need to get your horse. Can you stand?"

"If you put me down." She felt a mixture of fright, embarrassment, and shockingly anger.

He easily lowered her to her feet before he spurred his horse into a run that soon had him overtaking Princess. He reached out and grabbed the dangling rein, pulling the mare to him, and then slowing her enough to turn and bring her back to where Holly was dusting off her skirt even though it had yet to touch the road.

He leaned over his pommel as he studied her, and for the first time she got a good look at the tall man who had saved her from a bad fall or worse. "I... thank you," she said not feeling grateful even though she should.

When her gaze met his, she felt shocked at the handsome face—not young, not old, but an expression in those eyes that seemed older than the hills. She'd never understood what that meant, not until this moment.

His smile was crooked. "Riding sidesaddle seems a little stupid to me, if you'll pardon my saying it."

"It's what ladies do," she protested tightening her lips.

"Not those with the sense they were born with and who don't want to break their fool necks."

She didn't like him, but she would behave properly even if he didn't. "I don't know why she ran off with me," she managed, working to avoid the fuming words coming to mind. Good thing she had been raised polite—even if he clearly had had no such training.

Holly did not consider herself vain, but men generally responded to her looks. Her blonde hair, slim body, and finely boned face led to expected smiles and compliments. This man didn't see her as a beautiful woman or even as a woman. His expression had the same disapproval he might have shown a disobedient child

Determined to hide her irritation, as she was never rude—especially not when someone had done her a major favor, she managed a smile that she hoped was grateful—even while she felt anything but.

"I truly appreciate your help." She guessed her tone didn't sound contrite when she saw his smirk.

"That skirt could get caught by the wind?"

"No, hardly any breeze."

"You ridden her many times?"

"This is our first."

"And you started to gallop her but lost control?"

"No, I never intended... We had just turned back to the stable."

His smile didn't change. "You need somebody to ride her who knows how to handle a horse and teach her when she wants to go home, she can't race to do it."

"I've been taking lessons," she protested and couldn't stop the resentful tone.

"Whoever it was should have taught you about horses and barns. Next time you take her out, when you turn her toward her stall and oats, keep a better grip on the reins. Are you afraid to ride her now?"

"No." She looked around for a big rock to help her mount. He leaped from his horse, and she saw he was even taller than he had looked. "I'll lift you up," he said as he moved to her side.

She wanted to say no. She didn't want him touching her again. She still remembered how his powerful arm and hand had felt as he had reached out and lifted her from her saddle as though she had weighed nothing. She had no choice. She could never get up without help. She nodded with more irritation than she had a right to feel. "Will she run off again," she asked as she arranged herself on the saddle.

"I'll stay with you until you are back to the barn."

"I have her in a stable," she said forcing a smile. How could she repay him? Oddly enough, she felt more like giving him a slap. He had treated her as though she was a novice, a child, an inexperienced... Well, she was where it came to a horse.

With seemingly one fast step, he was back in his saddle and rode alongside her. It helped her to gain back the confidence she had lost. At the stable, she didn't object when he dismounted and lifted her down.

"I would like to give you a reward," she said. "I don't have money with me but if you..."

He stopped her with a raised hand. "No reward needed, ma'am." The sarcastic look was back. She wished she hadn't noticed how handsome he was. He wasn't young. There were lines on his cheek, and she saw around his eyes-- eyes used to looking toward the sun too often.

"I insist," she said.

"You can insist all you want, but I'm not taking money for doing what anyone would do in that situation."

Before she could argue, Perez came out from the stable. "You are back soon," he said as he took Princess' reins. He looked up then at the man who had remounted his horse. "I know you?" he asked.

"Antonio?"

Perez grinned. "Sí."

"Good to see you again." He tipped his hat and looked back at Holly. "Good day, ma'am. Consider riding astride next time. Ladies do many foolish things to be proper. It isn't much help in avoiding a broken neck." With that, he rode off without a backward glance.

She gritted her teeth against that desire to say something cutting—even if he couldn't hear. He made it difficult to remain a lady. "You seemed to know him. Who is that man?" she asked Perez as he led her horse back into the stable.

"Used to be a padre."

"A priest?" That didn't seem possible. The man had had a hard look to him. She had felt his cartridge belt against her body as he had lifted her in front of him. Where many men wore holsters, not many wore them low enough to need to be tied down as his had been.

"No, a padre. He is not now though." He led Princess into her stall and pulled off the saddle, which he carried to the saddle room.

"I want to care for Princess," she said as he removed the horse's bridle. She needed to learn to do all these things. Perez handed her a curry brush. After she had brushed the mare's coat for what she felt were sufficient minutes, she found a portion of oats to feed her.

At the gate, she turned and looked into the mare's eyes, petting her forehead, unsure what would make her happy. Maybe the swishing tail meant the same as it would in a dog. The horse had a pretty face, a lighter brown than the rest of her. Watching her now, the mare had one ear forward and the other moving as though trying to hear something.

"When she wags her tail, is that that the same as a dog?" she asked Perez, who was cleaning the nearby stall.

He shook his head. "Flies bother her. The ears though, that's what tells you a horse is listening. If they are back, she's angry." He studied her a moment. "She is trying to figure you out."

"Me too."

She smiled then and walked from the stable to her cottage. The ride hadn't gone well. On the other hand, she has survived. Maybe Ollie and the stranger had been right. She should stop worrying about being a lady and ride astride. She didn't have the natural balance and ease in the saddle of her friend, Grace. She could learn to handle a horse though. She would learn.

Vince Taggert drew his horse up to the hitching rail in front of Sicilla's General Store. He grinned, as he saw an automobile working its way down the street, startling his horse as well as all the burros and horses on Main Street.

He shook his head as the funny little horseless carriage managed to get past him and turn the corner. It would never catch on—too unreliable. He thought about lighting a cigarette but decided to go inside first.

The building was cool. Goods lined two sides with clearly a feminine and a masculine division of merchandise.

"Damnitall," Del Sicilla said as he came out from behind a counter. "John Damian. How the hell are you?"

Vince reached out to take his hand and then Connie Sicilla emerged from the other side to give him a big hug. "Welcome, friend."

"How about a drink?" Del suggested and ushered Vince back into their living quarters. In moments, the two were seated at the kitchen table and sipping good bourbon.

"Been awhile. What brings you back?" Del asked.

Connie entered, went to the stove, poured hot water into a tea pot before she sat at the table, her eyes on Vince. "It is good to see you. I didn't think you'd be here so soon... John."

He grinned watching her over the rim of his glass. "What, you don't like the name?"

"It would be fine for some men." She smiled with that witchy look she used when she wanted.

"It seemed a good idea. Do you know my real name since you know it's not John Damian?"

"No, but you never felt like a John to me."

"Ever think about telling your husband?" Del asked with a teasing grin. He turned his gaze on Vince. "If it's not John, what is it?"

"Vince... Vincent Taggert."

Although Connie didn't react to it, Del did. "One of the Taggerts?"

She looked at her husband. "That has significance?"

Vince nodded. "In some places it does."

Del sucked in a breath and let it out loudly. "So you were trying to avoid..." He didn't go on.

"All right," Connie said with exasperation. "I may lay claim to being a psychic of sorts, but I am not a mind reader." She gave a little laugh. "Explain."

"Not too complicated. I come from a family known for robbery, killing and scaring others into obeying whatever they demand. It began with my grandfather, Josiah, and his brothers... although likely further back."

"You are confusing me."

Vince smiled but felt no humor. "Most of the Taggert brand came from Kansas, Missouri, and Wyoming. No reason you'd hear about them down here. At least it's what I once thought." He looked at Del. "How do you come to know the name?"

"We've lived a lot of places, and gambling halls tend to gossip as much as a church full of women," Del said with a chuckle.

When Connie still looked perplexed, Vince said, "I've spent over twenty-five years trying to get away from that name."

"And gave up?" Del asked.

He shrugged. "In the end, it went with me name or not."

Del shook his head. "How'd you end up back here--right now?"

"The letter."

"I wrote him," Connie said. "I didn't think you'd be here this fast though."

Now it was Del's turn to look confounded as he

turned back to his wife. "Why?"

"And how did you know where I was?" Vince asked. He had mulled over the answer to that question as he had ridden south.

"You and Sam kept in touch."

"Now and again."

"When he and Abigail were in town, I asked if she knew how I could reach you. She didn't, but Sam overheard and asked why. He accepted my reason, and told me what he had last heard. I had no idea if you would still be there, of course. As to why, I argued with them over that."

"Sam and Abby?"

"No."

Vince leaned back in his chair and studied her. "Then who?"

"The voices." She smiled sheepishly. "I was worried about a friend and a proposed journey she is going to take. I felt concern as to the reliability of her friends. I asked the other side for whether it was safe and what to do. You kept coming up although it wasn't by name. It was the man in black, the man with the gun. I knew who they meant."

"You think this friend needed a man with a gun?"

She flushed. "I wasn't sure why you were their answer. I remembered though how you stood up for us when we were in Sutter Creek, and the mob was going to... well attack me for being a witch, or so they feared."

"I also remember how brave you and Del were. I doubt you needed me."

Connie shook her head. "That day you saved us from who knows what end. I also saw that while people respected you, stood back from you, you were also a man who wouldn't use a weapon-- if he didn't have to. That was maybe why they... wanted you. Or maybe not."

"You aren't making much sense, sweetheart," Del said.

Vince shook his head. "Seems a roundabout way to get help. Did you try warning your friend?"

"I did. She is stubborn. When she gets her mind made up, she goes straight for it. In this case, however, she has a good reason, one that I respect. Knowing that didn't worry me any the less."

"It can't be Abigail. Who then?" Vince asked.

Connie shook her head. "Holly Jacobs."

"The name doesn't ring a bell."

"She isn't from here. She arrived in Tucson to visit Grace. That was November of '99."

"She needs a gun hand why?"

Connie sighed. "I don't know that she needs that. She needs a guardian angel." She smiled then and levelly met his gaze.

"I am no angel, ma'am."

"You were to us that night."

"Well, don't mistake me for one. I may not be an outlaw, but many of the trappings that come with the Taggert name belong to me too. My weapons have gotten used a lot more than I could wish. I was in Sheridan because they offered me the job as deputy. I tried it, and it worked for awhile."

"They fired you?" Del asked.

"In a manner of speaking. The main problems in town had been straightened out." Or killed. "When a Colt is no longer needed, a man carrying it isn't either—especially after someone told who my family was."

"You ever try being a minister again?" Del asked. His expression seemed more contemplative than Vince would have expected.

"It seems I'm not much good at turning the other cheek." He smiled.

"There is an irony about this. Happens there is another Taggert in town." Del's words were succinct and his lips tight. It was Vince's turn to be taken aback, and he waited for the rest. "He was at the Pedrales last night. I heard his name from Ridge. He is also a man who stands out in a crowd—or maybe makes a crowd stand back. Ridge warned him to cause no trouble there, fingering his shotgun when he said it. Taggert only smiled with a look that is a lot like yours. I never thought about it at the time, but you two resemble each other. He's not as broad in the shoulders but tall with the same dark hair, rugged features."

"You get a first name?" He could hope they weren't closely related.

"He didn't offer it that I heard. I should add he had two hard cases with him. Maybe they were his brothers, but they didn't look like him—one sandy haired, mean eyes, short. The other middle height, balding young—a face nobody'd remember."

Vince smiled. "If you weren't a gambler whose business it was to remember."

Del nodded with an acknowledging grin. "Or a storekeeper. Anyway, those two use their guns a lot would be my guess. Not cowboys or storekeepers, if you get my drift."

Vince let out a breath. "The other mention what he was here for?"

"He was quiet, didn't say much, not the kind of man folks ask questions of."

"Great." He barely knew his three half-brothers. He had left home as early as he could get away. When he'd gone, the oldest would have been eight. Vince had taken off without even saying good-bye as he had believed it was the only way he'd get free. Asa, Cole and Jesse were vague memories. The one he remembered most was the oldest, Asa. Even at eight he had shown a cruel streak.

There'd on been one brief encounter, five years earlier, where he'd seen Asa and Cole. Asa might've grown to a man, but inside, clearly he hadn't changed. Cole gave away nothing of the man he was. Growing up with a father like theirs wasn't likely to be encouragement to become good men. If one of his brothers was in Tucson, he guessed he was about to find out which way the twig had been bent.

"Will you have supper with us?" Connie asked.

He shook his head. "Thanks, but I want to get my horse stabled, a hotel room and eat in town. The Rainbow still open?"

Del nodded. "You are welcome to bunk here."

"No, it should be a hotel, but I'll be back in the morning and... hear more about this problem. Any chance that in your shelves you have a suit and white shirt, maybe string tie?" He smiled at Connie as she nodded and led him to the store to show him a black suit that fortunately fit even his shoulders perfectly.

As he walked out of the store, he was aware Connie was still staring at him thoughtfully. He didn't want to know what she saw. There was no chance in hell that he'd ask her for one of her readings. He already knew his fate.